THE Comedian

A Novella

THE
Comedian

A Novella

STACY PARENTEAU

ISBN: 978-1-09837-780-9

First Edition.

Printed in the United States of America.

For Mom and Dad

1

Nobody in town could probably say when he first heard the name Emmon Mims or when he would hear it for the last time. He arrived as quietly as a summer breeze, melting the sleet of despair that had coated Dunville. By the time all was said and done, however, the citizens of Dunville would be yearning once again for the time before they crowned their comedy prince.

The tragedy of something broken and bleeding can never be understood without appreciating how it was once whole and shining. Only small towns can be ordinary and still be ridiculously charming, and it was hard to imagine a more ordinary town than Dunville, Massachusetts. The Dunville Congregational Church stood as the psychic fulcrum of the town, centering the diffused joy and peace radiating from the townspeople as they bustled about town running errands or rocked on their front porches after dinner. Almost everyone in town went to one of the three church services on Sundays, content in each other's company and bathed in God's love and light. While the church contained the heart and soul of Dunville, a myriad of small businesses provided the town with strong financial legs.

The biggest event in town every year was the Halloween pageant, wherein parents brought their children dressed in their most irresistibly adorable costumes, and adults had a chance to wear their own costumes, usually their favorite historical figure or movie character, and add some sparkle and glamour to their mundane suburban lives. But make no mistake—the 10,251 Dunville residents were happy people. Parents cheered their children at baseball and soccer games. They shoveled driveways for their elderly neighbors after a snowstorm. They worked hard, paid their bills, and raised their families. And their highest allegiance was to God. Until the new gods came. Laughter would heal what prayers had not.

Sleeping peacefully in a soft bend of the watery arm of the Charles River, Dunville was at first blissfully ignorant of the recession raging throughout the country, but its winds knocked the town over like a house of cards in the early fall of 2008. Businesses collapsed one by one; boards were nailed over the windows of diners and stores, which now stood as blinded, ghostly monuments in a town where misery was swamping the parents and children who had once spent carefree Saturdays eating and shopping and laughing. More and more people lost their jobs week after week, leaving them with nothing to do with their days but collect unemployment, wait for job offers that never came, try not to think about what they were going to do once their unemployment benefits ran out, and hold their Bibles close to their chests.

Clusters of people would surreptitiously hang around Dunville Market, lurking around the fruit stands, waiting keenly for the free food samples to be granted by the woman being paid twenty dollars a day to give cooking demonstrations, hoping nobody would figure out that their food stamps had run out for the week. The months snailed forward. Life slithered on, the fangs of fear and despair sinking deeper and deeper into people's souls. Many people in Dunville eventually resorted to visiting the food pantry in the next town, a humiliating action they had traditionally consigned to the "lazy-ass moochers" who clung to the lowest rung of the economic ladder; hunger always has a way of devouring even the fiercest pride. Parents continued to tuck their children in at night, trying their hardest to ignore the small growling bellies as they gave their goodnight kisses. They then went to their own bedrooms and burst into tears.

It started the way many things that turn out badly do—with the very best of intentions. In early 2009, one of Dunville's oldest and better-off residents, Charles McVay, decided to invest in a country club and a large supermarket to help recharge his enervated hometown. But his proudest achievement was to raise the corpse of a shuttered restaurant and reincarnate it as Dunville's first comedy club, The Dunville Jokebox; laughter was as good a business as any to help revive a dying town. The club opened in July 2009. Dunville residents who could pay the $10 entrance fee did so. The rest enjoyed a free night of comedians, both good and bad. Mostly bad.

In October, a young man showed up at the club with only a duffel bag containing three changes of clothes and all the necessary toiletries. Like most young comics, Emmon Mims had floundered in a sea of clubs, mostly playing in seedy strip joints and ghostly comedy clubs in Boston, where all three people in the audience were already asleep before Emmon even stepped onto the stage. He had heard about the new comedy club birthed and nurtured by Charles McVay in Dunville, and the idea of breathing laughter into a dying suburb scratched every romantic itch in his body. And McVay was paying a decent wage to comics trying to gain traction on the slippery road to glory and stardom.

At first, Emmon would play to only ten or so people a night.

He was not George Carlin, playing to sold-out concert halls. He was Emmon Mims, playing to a handful of Dunville citizens who could not stand to spend one more night in bed worrying about whether they will have enough money for groceries that week. He was their own little secret, their private, sweet love affair, and that was enough for them.

But nothing great can stay secret forever. Emmon's presence soon spread throughout Dunville as rapidly and quietly as a cold virus. Kids snuck out of their bedrooms and hoisted themselves up on the windowsills of the club to see Emmon, even as the temperatures dropped and snow began to whirl. People living in houses close to the club fell asleep to the sound of the fluffy laughter floating through the night air.

Emmon was a naturally gifted performer, but his jokes were not particularly brilliant. He joked about the economic hardship— fear loves to hold a mirror up to its face and see laughter staring back—but more than that, there was just something about Emmon to which the townspeople connected. His youth and energy were a flesh and blood elixir to people who felt like they had been sleeping in a graveyard for months on end.

If there was ever a man who was more loved than Emmon Mims was in those late evening hours, nobody in Dunville could name him.

2

As the people of Dunville fell in love with Emmon, he found something of his own to love. A few weeks after he started working at the club, Russ Manning, the club manager, hired Laura Hemmings as assistant manager. She was beautiful, but she either was not aware of her beauty or did not give it much merit—the best kind of beautiful. Emmon had seen dozens of topless dancers as he went from club to club, but nothing had touched him like his first sight of Laura. He started staying late at the club, writing jokes, whenever she was working late. He often walked by her office just to see the crack of light under her door.

One night, Emmon took a break when he was stumped for jokes and meandered into the club kitchen to raid the fridge; Laura walked in just as he was about to pop a plate of leftover spaghetti into the microwave. She saw Emmon and startled.

"Oh my God, I didn't know anyone was in here," Laura spouted. She smiled sheepishly as she recovered herself and walked over to the sink.

"Sorry, I didn't mean to scare you. I just got hungry," Emmon apologized as he blindly punched some numbered buttons on the microwave, his finger quivering as he did his best to look nonchalant as a swarm of butterflies fluttered around in his stomach.

"Can't think of any more jokes, huh?" Laura queried with a disarming smile as she poured her flat and stale coffee down the sink.

Emmon smiled broadly; his tension eased. *Smart and funny.* Oh yes, he liked this one.

"So, um, you're Laura, right?" he asked, knowing perfectly well what her name was.

"Yes. I just started here last month."

"I know."

Laura peeled a devilish smile. "Oh you do, do you?" she asked impishly.

Emmon quickly looked down at his feet, his cheeks flaring. "Well, um, yeah, I mean—"

"Yes, I guess you did know I was here. Otherwise you could just as easily write your jokes at home. And you would have no reason to hover around my office at night."

Laura smiled pleasantly, then turned and walked toward the door as Emmon watched after her, completely mortified.

"Well, still not many people in here, but the ones who are here seem happier than I've seen folks in a long time," Alice Appleby observed as she trickled sugar into her coffee cup at Fran's Flapjacks.

"Feels like this town is coming back to life. It's all getting better again, ever since Emmon Mims came here," Beth Baxter affirmed as she coated her chocolate chip pancake with translucent brown maple syrup.

Alice smiled slyly. "We all know you've got a thing for him, girlie."

Beth blushed and made a deep cut into her pancake. "No I don't. He's really funny. He's bringing more people into the club;

he's bringing in money. He's getting this town back on its feet, along with McVay's other investments."

Alice stared dully at Beth. "Yup, like I said, you're hot for him."

"Oh, shwutup," Beth commanded in an indignant garble as she grinded the fluffy bite of pancake with her dentures. "Better that women dream about him than about whether their families are going to end up in a shelter—or sleeping in their cars."

Alice stared at her companion for a minute, then gave a quick smile and sipped her coffee.

Emmon lay staring up at the clouds while Laura sat against a tree, bathing her feet in a pool of crinkly leaves. The wind rippled the velvety grass, and a group of ducklings bobbed on the crackling surface of the pond. Spring had begun to bestow its blessings.

"It looks like it's laughing," Emmon murmured as he gazed dreamily above.

"What?" Laura asked with a bemused look.

Emmon gestured toward the sky with his head. "That cloud, it looks like a dog that's laughing."

Laura looked up and smiled, the confused look on her face replaced by affectionate understanding. She looked back down at the leaves at her feet; she traced the dried veins of a pathetically desiccated leaf, an unburied corpse lingering from the winter months.

"This reminds me of summers when I was a kid; I would sit against a tree and read for hours in the woods."

"Was it that bad at home?" Emmon asked, only half-joking.

Laura continued to analyze the leaf with intense concentration. "My parents loved me. They wanted the best for me."

"Sounds like Hell."

Laura conceded a slight smile. "The only problem was 'the best for me' involved getting married right out of high school, like my mother and all of my aunts did, and staying in wonderful Hope Meadows, population twelve hundred, for the rest of my life. I got almost all straight As in high school, but nothing ever changed my parents' mind that my future should include nothing more than having a hardworking husband and staying home with my babies."

Emmon stared at her for a minute. "Well, you obviously didn't find a husband in high school." He smiled. "I'm glad."

Laura returned the smile. "No, I went to Boston University, even got a scholarship. Of course, Mom would call me every couple of weeks, asking if I had found a boyfriend yet."

"Well, did you?" Emmon queried abashedly.

Laura smiled and ruffled through the leaves at her feet. "No one serious. I was really focused on my studies. I ran track; I was involved in student government. I really wanted to be someone."

Emmon blinked softly and returned his gaze to the bloated clouds above. "I know the feeling."

Laura smiled. "I can't imagine you ever *not* being someone. You're everything to the people in this town."

"The people in this town need me and want me. It's like I was meant to be here. I'm not a mistake to them. I'm not an accident."

Laura looked at the miniature cloud puffs floating on Emmon's eyes, now darkened by a hard glare. She looked up at the dog cloud, and she could have sworn it was no longer laughing.

Emmon lay on his bed that night, staring up at the ceiling, hands clasped behind his head. He watched the fan blades slice through the musty air, the unrelenting whipping motion stirring his thoughts into a messy batter oozing in his head.

Laura. It was not a crush. It was not infatuation. It was not searing lust. It was as if a hand had reached down from Heaven and shaken his soul awake. Nothing in his life had touched him like Laura. His love for her was the most intense and purest thing he had ever known, like an incandescent white flame.

There was only one other thing that made Emmon feel as alive—the laughter from the audience. Every time he heard that laughter, it was like drinking a sweet tonic brewed in Heaven. Every time Emmon walked onto that stage and looked out at the audience, it was like the world had cracked open and all the love and goodwill it contained gushed forth like sweet milk from a coconut.

Soon it was more than just laughter he was drinking in. A straggle of townsfolk waited outside the club every week to see Emmon arrive. Men and women stopped him on the street to talk; there was nothing better to color the dourness of ordinary life than rubbing against fame and walking away with stardust on your sleeve.

Nobody could guess that beneath the laughter that lolled under the sweet glow of the club lights, fear, ego and greed were churning into an emotional cyclone that would raze the dignity and humanity of an entire town. Nobody had any idea that the town would soon become divided into winners and losers, heroes and villains, lovers and haters.

That July, The Count began.

3

The conversation from early last month was permanently carved in Laura's brain, like the juvenile pronouncements of love etched on dilapidated old trees, and replayed in her mind as she and Emmon watched two seagulls tussle over a charred hot dog lying limply in the bronze sand.

"People in this town have never been happier, Russ," Laura declared to her boss.

"Exactly the problem. Hate has always been more profitable than love. People don't pay to watch two dogs lick each other's face; they will pay to watch two dogs fight to the death." Russ paused. "People always need to have a winner and a loser."

"We make those people happy. And this town is starting to recover."

"They take from the guys on the stage, just as the guys take from the audience. But we can give them something more." Russ twisted his lips into a wry smile. "There is one thing that is never going out of style."

Laura lowered her eyes. "War."

"Yes, war." Russ smiled keenly. "Smart girl."

"So we're really doing it?" Laura asked warily.

"These dogs will maul each other to death," Russ responded with the satisfaction of a snake that has just swallowed a rodent whole.

Laura slowly looked up to meet her boss's eyes. "When will it start?" she asked quietly.

"Next month."

Emmon and Laura lay to the side of the sand dune, frittering the July afternoon away watching the mercurial seagulls and the sparkly water and the frothy waves crack and creep onto the shore.

"See any laughing dog clouds today?" Laura asked with a suppressed smile.

"Not yet," Emmon responded quietly as he gazed above.

Laura turned to look at him. "What's wrong?"

"I was just thinking about this kid in school. He always got the lead in the school plays. He was good too. Then I saw my first comedian when my friend Joe and I snuck out to a comedy club one night. We watched through the window. I remember wondering what it must feel like to have all those people literally at your feet, being the only person in their world, even if just for twenty minutes."

"Well, how does it feel?"

"It was the greatest feeling in the world at first. Nobody had ever paid attention to me for two minutes, let alone twenty."

Laura stared at him.

"But it feels a little lonely sometimes too, being up there alone in the spotlight. The audience never thinks about what it feels like for their idols, just so long as they go to sleep happy."

"Do you still feel lonely?"

Emmon looked at Laura and smiled gently. "Not as much as I used to."

He wanted her completely now, his desire scalding his insides, jolting him awake in a cold sweat night after night. He turned toward her. He kissed her shiny forehead and then pecked the tip of her nose. He felt as nervous as he did the first time he ever took to the stage, his throat as dry as the sand burning his toes. Laura unlaced her blouse and Emmon slid down his pants as a bulging cloud passed over the intrusive eye of the searing sun.

The idea for The Count was simple enough. Each of the twenty competing comedians took to the stage for twenty minutes, twelve nights a month for a year. Laura made up the monthly performing schedule and sent a copy to Randy Yellowmander, editor of *The Dunville Scooper*, the town's daily newspaper, to publish prior to the start of each month. Laura took the head count of the audience for each comedian every night, Monday through Saturday; seating capacity was one hundred. A maximum of ten comedians were scheduled to perform each night. At the end of the month, the nightly counts for each comedian were tallied and sent to Yellowmander to publish in *The Scooper* at the beginning of the next month. The prize after one year of competition for the top performer after all of the months were added—money. Of course, money. One hundred thousand dollars to be exact, signed over by Charles McVay himself.

It was not long before Emmon started to feel the oven-hot swelter of competition. Comedians from all over Boston hopped as merrily as drunken toads to Dunville for a spot at The Jokebox after Russ Manning advertised the contest in the major Boston newspapers at the beginning of June. Emmon and one of the other regular club performers, Bill Dickens, were entered in the first-year competition, along with eighteen other hopefuls who had been chosen from over fifty comedians who had auditioned for Russ and Laura. Bill stood out from the rest of the comedic pack with his caustic intellectual humor, but he might as well have been delivering his jokes in Mandarin for the majority of Dunville citizens, most of whom were more interested in nightly sitcoms and the monthly pie-eating contests in town than in philosophical debates and global politics. The Bible was the only book that could be found in the homes of most Dunville residents, but even that sacred tome, though held very dear, went largely unread, buried at the bottom of the drawers of countless nightstands. Most people in town were offended at Bill's religious jokes. All they knew was they loved God; they did not want to see Him sliced and diced by the razor-sharp jokes of a haughty, highbrow comedian. But some in town, mostly the educated, professional men and women who commuted into Boston for work, were magnetized by Bill's humor and had been going to the club at least once a week to see him perform.

Other than Bill, however, Emmon had never had to compete for Dunville's attention during his first nine months at the club. The two star comedians were typically scheduled to perform five nights a week, with Emmon performing on Monday, Wednesday and Friday nights and Bill on Tuesday and Saturday nights. There were only a handful of other comedians at the burgeoning club, most of them guys who had always lived in Dunville and were looking to make some money but were mainly allowed to perform only as brief warm-up acts for Bill and Emmon or on Thursday night when neither of the two headliners performed. Bill was Emmon's only real competition, but it was Emmon most citizens came out to see. It was more than cranking out jokes; the people of Dunville seemed to see a part of themselves in Emmon. It was that rare occurrence when the

14

flesh was stripped and souls connected.

Now Emmon was fighting with nineteen other comedians for Dunville's soul. The monthly dogfight at The Jokebox was clearly the most exciting thing ever to happen for Dunville residents. Even the news of Jada McKinna's kidnapping in May fizzled as quickly as a shooting star once The Count got underway. It was one of those tragedies people never expect to happen in quiet suburbia—a sweet-faced girl in ponytails kidnapped while walking the two blocks from the bus stop to her house. Randy Yellowmander featured countless articles in *The Scooper* speculating about Jada's fate, replete with quotes from nameless witnesses who did not really see anything because they did not really exist. Every week there was a new story in *The Scooper*. Jada McKinna had been murdered. She had been sold into child slavery. She was being held in the kidnapper's basement, starved and raped daily. But as the weeks went by, the headlines about Jada's kidnapping got smaller and smaller, dwarfed by larger and larger headlines about the happenings at the club. *The Scooper* featured a front-page story on Emmon after he had finished in first place in the July ratings, with Bill Dickens finishing a distant second—a fact that Yellowmander was sure to highlight in the article.

Emmon never thought he would be on top anywhere. Growing up in Worcester, Massachusetts, he always seemed to be trampled on at the bottom. His mother discovered she was pregnant soon after she had turned forty-five and his oldest brother had just turned twenty-one, and Emmon always sensed resentment simmering beneath the joyful glee that emanated from his mother when people told her how lucky she was to have another "blessing." He would sometimes catch his mother flinch in embarrassment when strangers looked at them, probably assuming he was her grandson. His father would often come home tired and harried, sagging under the weight of having to now support another child, just when he was soon to be relieved of his breadwinning duties.

Emmon would do juggling and hula hoop acts for his parents in the living room, hoping his adorable incompetence would thaw their frozen parental instincts. The attempts always fell short. He would catch his mother looking out the window, perhaps imagining some magical place she could be if she were not imprisoned in a loveless marriage that had given her four children who daily scraped the perfect picture of motherhood she had painstakingly painted. His father would roll his eyes every five minutes, look at his watch, and ask with an irritated sigh, "Okay, is that it?" Emmon finally gave up, looking everywhere else he could for some tonic to fill the emptiness inside. Eventually, he found it.

Emmon's best friend, Joe Mika, talked him into sneaking out of Joe's house one night to check out the new comedy club in the neighboring town. They were too young to be admitted into the club, so they settled for peeking through the side window. The club was gaining much-needed publicity due to the recent addition of topless dancers, but Emmon fell in love with only one thing: the laughter from the audience. He decided right then that laughter would soon be his.

Emmon was an average student in school and had no real desire to go to college, but his parents would not stop nagging him until he sent in some college applications. He grudgingly enrolled at Johnson & Wales, but none of his courses held even the slightest interest for him. Emmon's father gave him a sullen glare when he announced he was dropping out of college to hit the comedy clubs, but Emmon promised he would go back to college in the event his newfound career did not pan out. He moved to Boston and started at the smallest clubs. Unable to afford an apartment, he would sleep in the back room of the clubs along with other obscure but hopeful comics, who often stayed up late into the night gushing about their favorite topless dancers.

Emmon learned only one word of the language of the comedy club circuit: win. He wanted to be the brightest star in the comedy galaxy, no matter whom he had to nuke in order to shine. Smiles was the first club at which he worked. He put garlic pepper on Jim Crouch's hamburger, causing him to break out in hives and miss his act. Emmon stepped in and became the hero of the night. Heroes are soon forgotten, however, without repeated acts of heroism. Emmon was again gracious enough to step in when Fred Chuck had to miss his act after his car stalled because someone had put water in his gas tank and he could not afford to call a tow truck. Emmon soon became known as the most dependable comic at every club he worked. Nobody saw the dark underbelly of ambition jutting out beneath the man who seemed as affable and charming as a puppet. As for Emmon, he was always secretly hoping that if his sins ebbed far enough away into the past, the waves of forgiveness would lap them up and drown them in the vast ocean of human frailties. But whenever he heard the laughter from the audience, he finally knew what it was to feel loved.

Now he was Emmon Mims, redeemer and reigning comedy king of a dying Boston suburb. It was easier to entrance an audience full of desperate people in a placid suburb than an audience full of drunk and rowdy people in the seedy clubs in Boston. The more people needed to laugh, the less was needed to make them laugh.

People who are drifting helplessly in the water will watch a giddy dolphin flipping and flirting for hours, anything to avoid thinking about drowning. Emmon's charm was magnetic, an emotional fire stick that rekindled the dying embers of hope and joy in Dunville. He wondered in his quiet moments, however, just how long the audience would love him, and how long he could hold on to fame's coattails.

4

Emmon stared at the yellowed newspaper encased in the glass frame on the wall.

"An original issue of the 'Dewey Defeats Truman' paper," Randy Yellowmander, chief editor of *The Dunville Scooper*, stated in response to Emmon's mental observation.

Emmon smiled. "So why did you ask me here?"

"Because I think we can help each other out," Yellowmander responded with a keen expression that made Emmon's stomach spasm. "Two months now you've won in the ratings—looks like you'll win September too." He paused. "The peeps feel like you understand them. That's the most important thing for a comedian, even more than the jokes themselves."

"Well?"

A wry smile marred Yellowmander's otherwise smooth, attractive face. "But even that isn't enough. It's not just who you are as a comedian. People are always looking for a hero—someone to believe in. They have to believe in you as a *person*." He paused and gazed thoughtfully at Emmon. "Dickens did better in August than he did in July."

"So what do you want me to do, start kissing babies? Helping old ladies across the street?" Emmon asked flippantly.

"Yes—and we'll be there to snap the picture."

"Even Dunville residents can't be that stupid," Emmon responded warily.

Yellowmander blinked in surprise and then gave that wry smile again. "Never ceases to amaze me how much contempt idols have for their minions," he murmured.

Emmon stared at him, hot anger seeping into his bones.

"People are like the guppies in that tank," Yellowmander continued, strutting his head toward the oversized fish tank in the corner of his office. "They'll eat up whatever we drop in front of them. They don't think—they eat."

"You wouldn't sell many of your so-called newspapers if they did think."

Yellowmander bristled but then smiled knowingly. "We both need the guppies."

Emmon smiled in return, his fondness growing with each passing minute. "So I help a stranded motorist once in a while, and the wonderful hicks of Dunville read about it, and I keep my high ratings. And Bill Dickhead gets left in the dust."

"You got it, my good man. We will show the good citizens of Dunville the good and the bad."

The smirk on Emmon's face morphed into a bemused frown. "The bad?"

"You tell the jokes, Emmy; I'll slit the throats." Yellowmander smiled. "And you drink the blood."

"And what do you get?"

"A quarter of your prize money—twenty-five thousand dollars."

Emmon blinked softly, a wry smile cracking his face. "I

should've known."

"Aw, don't look so sad, Emmy. I mean, this was never about the money, was it?"

In the almost three months since The Count began, something had started to change in Dunville. It was as though some dark and foul fumes had spewed forth from the sewers and suffocated all of the decency and goodwill that had once permeated Dunville. It was a depravity worse than the economic hardship that had hit the town two years ago. Stomachs may have been empty then, but souls were still full and intact.

The Jokebox had helped revitalize Dunville and was now turning a handsome profit. The club employed local people in various capacities. The club was packed on nights when Emmon performed. More people than ever had swamped the club since The Count began, wanting to play a role in creating a winner. The club brought in money, which spilled over into other businesses.

Dunville was recovering from the indignity of economic collapse, but a new sickness was starting to take hold—a meanness, a ruthlessness. Dunville citizens felt the fangs of competition pierce their skin and inject hateful venom into their blood. The same people who once ate together after church and watched each other's children now looked at each other with malice and antipathy.

Emmon certainly had his devoted fans, but so did Bill Dickens, though in fewer numbers, and it was not long before the citizens of Dunville felt like they had to pledge their loyalty to one or the other. A sharp black line had been drawn, the way competition always draws a line. There would be a winner and a loser—and nobody wants to be a loser.

Phil Rigley was forced to drop out of The Count and leave Dunville at the end of October. He did not have the star status of Emmon, or even Bill Dickens, but he had moved up to the top five in the September ratings, and he was carving out a small but loyal following. Then Randy Yellowmander published a story in *The Dunville Scooper* in mid-October about how Phil had been convicted of a sex crime in his hometown of Cranston, Rhode Island, two years ago. The story was true enough, but the edges of the entire truth had been cut off, leaving a maimed, deformed version of the story strewn on the pages of *The Scooper*.

One night in college, Phil had gotten drunk at a frat party and then went back to his parents' house. He urinated in his neighbor's bush instead of waiting until he got inside his house. Unfortunately, the lady of the house was neurotic when it came to her children, and she called the police claiming Phil had deliberately exposed himself. His neighbors had friends "in high places," and Phil was just a college student. He served one year in jail. He did not go back to college after serving his time, deciding instead to try his hand at comedy. He could be a free agent and play at clubs that did not bother to do background checks. Phil had considered changing his name, but he was his parents' only child, and he felt obligated to carry on the family name. He had been scurrying from one ratty comedy club to the next in Boston when he saw the advertisement for The Count in early June. He auditioned and was officially entered into the contest at the end of June. His audience grew each month, and for the first time in a long time, he felt accepted, even if he did constantly feel overshadowed by Emmon Mims and, to a lesser extent, Bill Dickens.

But Randy Yellowmander dug for past dirt like an anteater digs for ants. He discovered Phil's past arrest while rummaging through old online newspaper stories in Cranston and then verified his conviction through an online court records portal. Yellowmander showed Emmon the sordid treasures he had unearthed, and they high-fived each other after Emmon had finished reading. They now had one less competitor to worry about.

Things turned very ugly for Phil Rigley after the story appeared in *The Scooper*. Attendance at his acts plummeted. Phil walked out of his apartment one morning to see "PEDOPHILE" spray-painted across his car. He came home one day and froze after he closed the door. He could see the outline of a form twirling from the ceiling in the dim light. He felt his hand flip the light switch. He could not even swallow; it felt as though a huge invisible hand had reached out and clenched his throat. Suspended from the ceiling fan, at the end of a tattered rope, was a black-and-white baby goat. Its downy ears hung like puffy little curtains, masking green eyes staring blankly ahead like the eyes of a stuffed animal. Taped to the goat's fur was a sign that read "Kiddie Raper."

Phil packed his bags, paid his landlord the next month's rent in advance, and drove back to Cranston, the only true home he had ever known, praying that at least the people there had forgiven him.

The salt nightlight flooded the sparse, dingy basement room in the comedy club with soft mustard light. Emmon lay on the cratered mattress, his head nestled in the crook of his bent arm. The muted laughter from above sounded as sweet to Emmon as the rustling leaves that had lulled him to sleep when his parents were too tired, or simply forgot, to read his favorite books to him. Emmon propped his head on his hand and gazed out the window across the room, willing the moonlight to vaporize the lonely feeling that seethed like acid inside.

"What are you thinking?"

Emmon looked down at Laura as she stirred softly beside him. He smiled gingerly. "Nothing important."

"Are you nervous about the new jokes tomorrow night?" Laura asked, tracing her finger down the side of his face.

"No. I've been holding steady—in first place the past four months. We're already halfway through November and I've got the lead."

Laura grimaced. "That's the most important thing now, isn't it?"

"Circling every win on my calendar," Emmon confirmed with a whimsical smile, though Laura was sure she saw the faintest shadow of a sneer.

"Well, there's something else for you to think about now," she whispered, circling her finger slowly around her belly button.

Emmon stared intently out the window, his eyes hardened with an emotion Laura did not even want to try to name.

"Emmon?"

He blinked and lowered his eyes, his lips loosening into a velvety smile. "I know." He placed his hand on Laura's stomach, her womb quivering beneath her pearl white camisole.

"It doesn't feel real yet," Laura murmured as the laughter upstairs waned with the end of the act.

Emmon blinked softly. "Sometimes it's the only thing that does feel real to me." He stared out the window. "Those people come out and see me night after night. They love me, but do they really care about me? And the women, the way they look at me—I know what they want." He looked back down at Laura. "But all I want is

24

to lie here, next to you, night after night."

Tears filled Laura's eyes as Emmon smothered his face in her hair, splayed across the pillow in silken ginger rivulets.

Laura tried to dismiss the cramping and fatigue last month as the insidious by-products of overwork, as she had been using birth control pills, but walls constructed by delusion crumble all too easily. She made an appointment with her doctor, her hands quivering as she dialed. She sat in the waiting room three days later, gazing out the window at the bluebird bopping on the naked branch quavering in the raw, merciless wind. She had a new life inside of her—she already knew it—yet she had never felt more alone. She was supposed to feel happy, blessed, but she felt an emptiness so deep inside she was afraid it would suffocate the baby. Laura did not know exactly what life was going to be like from now on, but of one thing she was certain: everything she had been in her life, everything she had achieved, was now winnowed down to one identity—mother.

Then there were the rumors floating around the club. Emmon was working with Randy Yellowmander to stage opportunities for Emmon to come along and rescue a hapless motorist, with his heroic act then photographed and glorified in *The Scooper*. Emmon had colluded with Yellowmander to dig up dirt on Phil Rigley. Laura did her best to ignore it all; love comes with free blinders. But she could see the truth seeping through like moonlight through pale curtains. How long can even the brightest love stay blind? She had seen it from the beginning, squirming like slimy worms beneath the resplendent grass. Emmon could not live with losing; it would be like killing a part of his soul. His ambition was like a fierce horde of mice, unrelentingly gnawing away at his moral flesh. How much longer before only a cold, clunky, soulless skeleton remained? Could she stand by Emmon no matter what he did? "Support your husband and raise him up," Laura's mother and aunts had always preached. But did everyone deserve unconditional love? Did any man believe he could just put his sins under his pillow at night and find his soul there in the morning, put there by the fairy who magically rights all wrongs in the world, turns all wrongdoings into dust that blows into the placid, merciful sky?

5

December had walked in on tiptoe, as if it knew that Dunville was not quite ready for the official start of winter. Emmon sat at his wobbly kitchen table late in the month reading the article in *The Dunville Scooper* for the fifth time, a queasy feeling worming around in his stomach. He had helped yet another elderly couple whose car had broken down last week, and Randy Yellowmander included a short article on Emmon's heroics in *The Scooper*, complete with fake quotes from Emmon about how important it was to help others and spread kindness in one's community. Randy did not write about how Emmon had put water in the couple's gas tank and then followed them as they pulled out of their driveway, ready to be there with helping hands when their car started to mysteriously sputter, with Randy hiding in the backseat with his camera.

Emmon had never once had his name in print before coming to Dunville; he had always felt like he never fully existed. His oldest brother handed his perfection down the line to each of his three younger brothers, leaving it worn and tattered by the time it reached Emmon. He tried reading his first book when he was six, but nothing on the pages made any sense to him. The words looked like tiny black ants marching across the pages. His parents sat stiffly in their seats while Emmon's teacher explained to them that their son might have a learning disability. They were careful to avoid meeting the teacher's eyes, simmering with resentment that they now had a child who would never attain academic glory. Emmon frequently met his father's angry eyes in the mirror on the way home. His parents begrudgingly took him to a specialist, a brisk, conscientious man in an expensive dark suit who diagnosed Emmon with something called dyslexia. He started receiving "retard tutoring," as the kids at school called it. His parents did not talk about it at all. Emmon would hear the teachers at school joke about how he must have received the "defective gene" that somehow skipped over all of his brothers and showed up in him. Other teachers would chide him for being "lazy" and trying to coast by on his older brothers' academic achievements. Emmon worked hard to understand the words on the page, trying to prove to his parents and teachers that he could do anything his brothers had done. Eventually, the words did start to make sense. No amount of remediation, however, could obliterate the sense of shame and worthlessness that had been branded on his psyche.

Only under the bright spotlight did the gremlins lurking in his memory scurry to the shadowy recesses of his mind. Emmon was magnetized by the limelight after sneaking out to the comedy club with Joe Mika and seeing the audience light up with laughter. He would toss out a joke or flip comment in the middle of class, a proclivity that finally earned him the adoration of his fellow students but also several detentions. Once Emmon embarked on his stand-up career, his heart glowed like a red fluorescent rock whenever he looked out at the people who were clearly charmed by his personality and stage presence, if not particularly impressed with all of his jokes. Then he arrived in Dunville and became the star comic at The Jokebox, and he quickly luxuriated in his newfound local fame. He later reveled in seeing the headlines in *The Scooper* at the beginning of each month touting his victory in the previous month's ratings once The Count started. And Emmon delighted in seeing the stories and pictures Randy Yellowmander published illuminating his staged altruistic deeds, even if his delight was somewhat jaundiced by a queasy feeling in his gut.

This is the last time, Emmon promised himself as he finally put the paper down. He took a couple of Tums, put on his favorite shirt and slacks, and headed to the club. He was on track to winning the December ratings.

Emmon bounced down the basement steps and headed toward the small utility room with the cratered mattress at the opposite end of the basement. He stopped abruptly when he saw Laura leaning against the wall.

"Laura, what's wrong?"

Her shoulders started to shake.

"Is it the baby?" Emmon queried urgently.

Laura turned around. "Yes, the baby. It's always the baby. My mother and aunts and sisters call me almost every day to ask about the baby. Is my morning sickness bad? Do I want a boy or a girl? Have I thought about names? And just wait until I start to show more—everyone in town will be patting my stomach before they even ask for your autograph."

Emmon furrowed his eyebrows. "Laura, what is it?"

"I don't even know who I am anymore," Laura breathed. She wiped away a tear.

Emmon relinquished a soft smile. "I know that feeling," he said quietly.

Laura gazed at him. "You know how I'm known in this town? 'Emmon Mims's girlfriend.' I don't want to be known as anyone's girlfriend." She paused, a reproachful glare shadowing her face. "Least of all yours, these days."

A slight look of shame jaundiced Emmon's face as he shifted his gaze to a spider inching up the wall.

"Don't ask what I'm talking about," Laura said in a tight voice.

"I wasn't going to," Emmon responded softly, his eyes still fixed on the ascending spider.

"It's not enough for you to shine; you have to snuff everyone else out too."

"I can't lose. Ever. I feel like I've lost all my life," Emmon whispered in a cracked voice as he looked back at Laura. "But I love you. I *love* you, Laura. When I first heard laughter from an audience, it was magic. It's like I had been living in a dark room all my life, and someone suddenly parted the curtains and opened the window. Everything was bright and fresh, like how a baby must first see things when it's born. I basked in it. I soaked it up. But as much as I loved it, I knew it wasn't real. The people in the audience are faceless puppets, laughing when I want them to. But when I held you for the first time, when I first made love to you, I finally had something *real*. You and that baby inside of you are the only real things I have ever known."

Laura gazed at Emmon with a queer expression that spiked every hair on the back of his neck. She looked down at the floor and swallowed hard. "Emmon, it's gone."

"What are you talking about? What's gone?" Emmon's stomach began to tauten the way it does when one slowly drinks in an unpleasant reality.

Laura found the courage to look Emmon in the eyes. She had always had plenty of courage. "The baby. It's gone. Last week I . . . I . . ." A tear trickled down her face. "Well, let's just say you've lost."

Emmon bit his lower lip, his body burning with the kind of anger one can never give voice to. He turned around and looked out the window at the other end of the basement. Laura stared at him for a minute and then slowly walked up the basement stairs to her office.

Bill Dickens walked down to the basement and approached Emmon as he was crossing a huge red "X" over the last day of the month on the oversized calendar taped to the wall between the stairs and utility room.

"The December ratings come out tomorrow," Emmon blurted, more to himself than to Bill.

"It doesn't matter for you anymore, Emmon."

Emmon gave him a sharp sideways glare. "What are you talking about?"

"You're going to drop out, Emmon. You're going to leave town and go home to care for your sick mother. That will really touch their hearts."

"Why would I drop out when I'm number one?"

"Because if you don't, everyone in town will know what Laura did to your baby a couple of weeks ago." Bill smiled, the ends of his mouth twisting up into mean curves. "You guys apparently forgot that some of the rest of us also like to go into that sweet little room sometimes and take a nap on that crappy mattress," Bill taunted with a quick, merciless wink. He stole a quick look through the opened door of the utility room to ensure that it was presently empty.

Emmon felt like a steel hand had reached through his chest and squeezed his heart.

"How do you think the good citizens of Dunville will feel about you once they learn your girlfriend had an abortion? Forgiveness has its limits, you know."

"But blackmail doesn't, apparently," Emmon spat bitterly.

Bill smirked. "Oh right, I forgot—only *you* are allowed to destroy people's lives. God has *His* limits when it comes to forgiving, right?"

Bill could have sworn he saw a twinge of shame flit across Emmon's face, but if Emmon had felt any shame, it was now impossible to discern beneath his cold, hard stare.

Emmon lowered his head. "Tell anyone you want. It wasn't my abortion."

Bill now lasered Emmon with his own cold, hard stare. "Even if you suffer nothing, you know how they'll feel about Laura. She'll be lucky if they let her leave this town quietly. I know you don't care about much, Emmon, but one thing I know—you care about Laura."

Emmon lifted his head and looked Dickens squarely in the eyes. "Tell them what you want. Laura's strong—she'll survive. But I need to survive too."

Bill smiled. "You're full of it. You aren't going to let me hurt Laura. And even if I do spill the beans, you won't be able to watch Laura suffer. You'll leave town the minute you see her sitting all alone at church."

Emmon was not full of it. He did not drop out of the contest and leave town, even when his mother really did become so ill with the flu she could not get out of bed. Bill kept his promise, too. His original plan was to tell his girlfriend Miranda and some of his friends in town about Laura's abortion in the hopes that the rumor would mushroom like a nuclear cloud. Upon careful reconsideration, however, Bill decided he needed a more powerful bomb. Rumors were like puppets; they did not fully come alive without a strong hand to prop them up. But he needed to be extra careful—the bigger the bomb and explosion, the greater the risk of getting caught. He did not want anyone to be able to trace the bomb back to him, lest he appear as sleazy as some people were beginning to perceive Emmon. Bill concluded that nothing would cause a greater visceral explosion than seeing Laura's name on actual medical documents pertaining to the abortion. He watched several online videos with clear instructions for picking locks and windows. He drove to a department store over eighty miles out of town to buy gloves and a ski mask, for which he paid cash—no trail of sleaze. Bill broke into Laura's apartment in the third week of January when he knew she was at the club and rummaged through her desk until he found a copy of her signed consent form for the abortion—exactly what he was hoping to find. He made some copies of the form on his home printer and posted them around town in the middle of the night. Now everyone knew what Laura considered to be the darkest secret of her life.

And Emmon was right. His fans did not hate him. They hated Laura. She had hurt Emmon Mims, a man whom many Dunville citizens would have elected to sainthood without hesitation. Sharp, disgusted glares lasered Laura everywhere she went. Each Sunday people cleared out of the pew she decided to sit in at church. Someone even left a mutilated beanie baby on the hood of her car.

Laura could not guess who had broken into her apartment and posted the consent form. As angry as Emmon was, she could not believe he would hurt her this way. She conjectured that it was one of Emmon's obsessed female fans who sometimes stalked her. Or maybe it was one of Emmon's competitors. The police questioned several people at the club, including Bill Dickens, who turned out to be as skilled at feigning innocence as he was at crafting jokes. The police had no witnesses, fingerprints or DNA evidence; nothing could be proven except Laura's shame and disgrace. Humiliated as she was, however, Laura never even once entertained the thought of leaving Dunville. She would stay and fight.

6

Anna Burrows could not remember exactly why she had decided to become a teacher, except that her mother was always pushing her to be either a teacher or a nun. The nun option, however, did not hold much appeal ever since Sister Jude had yelled at her for throwing up in biology class in high school, and then she started to question her whole faith after Father Murphy had put his hand on her thigh while having lunch with her family one Saturday afternoon.

Anna ultimately decided to major in history at Suffolk University and started teaching at Dunville High School right after graduation. At first, it felt like she had walked right into a schoolhouse scene from the *Little House on the Prairie* books. Students were well-behaved and kindhearted. There were, of course, the usual unsightly pits cratering the high school terrain. Girls occasionally unleashed nasty rumors when their feelings were hurt, and boys sometimes stood by their lockers and catcalled girls they liked. And there were some students who just did not like each other. For the most part, however, the students had formed a strong and nurturing commune, a colony of fledgling adults growing and developing and establishing themselves on the small planet of Dunville.

The economic collapse over two years ago only glued the students more closely to each other; students set up a food pantry at the school, bringing in tuna fish, peanut butter, juice and canned vegetables every week. They covered each other when someone could not afford to buy lunch on a particular day. Stomachs rumbled during class. Shoes were worn down to the heels; the same shirts and jeans were worn over and over again. But compassion had formed a strong and soft web that arched over the school, netting the fear and despair teeming among the students.

With Emmon Mims's arrival in town, hope and joy spread among the students more quickly than a flame in a forest. Nobody under eighteen was ever allowed in The Jokebox, but students gathered underneath the windows of the club, taking in Emmon's jokes as eagerly as a squirrel popping acorns into its mouth. They would tell their parents they were going to the mall, but even the parents knew that cover story was as flimsy as corn silk. They did not care; they could not bear the worried looks on their children's faces as they clawed through the weeks, grabbing each paycheck with shaky fingers. Their children were scared, and nothing vaporizes fear as quickly as laughter, so if they broke the rules to see Emmon Mims, then so be it.

Then it all changed. The Count began at the club, and the stench of competition permeated the hallways and classrooms. Emmon was the mainstream favorite, but Bill Dickens had his ardent supporters, mostly Honors students who worshipped Dickens's intellectual humor and wit and disparaged Emmon's "bubble gum" jokes. One morning while walking toward her classroom, Anna heard a couple of the Honors students jeering at two students in her American History class, denouncing them as "stupid fucks" with brains the "size of a pea." Her students spat back that Emmon was "The King" and only "fucking losers" would support a comedian who came in second month after month.

Anna would watch this scene replay over and over; she was an audience member again and again in a play she had never wanted to attend and had come to hate. Now she was almost starting to wish she had chosen the nun route. However much Anna's faith had wavered over the years, she still believed God could be found at church. He seemed to be abandoning Dunville more with each passing day.

Emmon looked out at the crowd from behind the musty velvet curtain and watched the people in the audience for a few minutes. He suddenly became aware of another person standing on the opposite end of the curtain, gazing out at the audience as she leaned against the wall. It was Laura. Emmon walked over to her.

"Looks like it'll be a pretty full house tonight," Emmon tentatively conjectured as he stared at the ginger curls tumbling over Laura's shoulders.

Laura nodded slightly. "I haven't taken the head count yet, but it looks like there are about twenty or so empty seats," she observed as she continued to look out at the audience.

A troubled look shadowed Emmon's face. "Used to be a packed house every single night."

Laura smiled wryly. "Don't worry, Emmon; people don't give up their saviors easily."

A tender expression dispelled the shadows from Emmon's face. "Do you hate them?"

Laura looked askew at Emmon. She slowly turned to face him. "Jealous of them," she responded with a half-smile.

"They only get a part of me, Laura. The part they need to get through the rest of the night." He paused. "They need to see a part of themselves up on that stage."

Laura gazed at him. "And you have to be the one to give it to them."

"You know I do. Those laughs from that audience are like trickles of water to a man parched in the desert."

"Or poison."

Emmon looked Laura squarely in the eyes. "Not ever going to love any other woman." His stare softened. "Nobody else is going to have me the way you did."

Laura looked at him keenly. "Did you love me, Emmon? Or was I just another thing you wanted to win?"

Emmon furrowed his eyebrows. "You really have to ask me that, Laura? You really believe you were nothing but a game to me?"

Laura stared blankly at him.

Emmon swallowed hard; his throat felt like it was lined with a fuzzy carpet. "I, uh, I have to go on now," he muttered as Russ Dickens finished his usual opening remarks and summoned Emmon to the stage.

"Of course, you don't want to keep them waiting—might cost you some points," Laura quipped as she turned back to stare out at the audience.

Emmon glared at her and then put on his brightest smile and took to the stage as effortlessly as a knight mounting a horse.

Marlon Grey had never considered himself a violent man. He still did not consider himself such, even as he sat at his computer searching for instructions on how to use a handgun. No man or woman is defined by just one act, and it would take less than a minute to do the deed. Less than a minute, and a life would be over. Marlon's fingers froze over the keys; he stared at his reflection in the screen for a minute. His thoughts then scurried to a place in his mind where no second thoughts were allowed to follow, and he continued his search for the clearest instructions on how to successfully fire a handgun.

Emmon lay on the cratered mattress watching the pigeon swagger along the windowsill. The last comedian for the night had just finished his act upstairs, and the only sound Emmon could hear was his own breathing. It was now the end of January, and he was still holding the ratings lead at the club. He was still winning. Yesterday he saw some schoolchildren wearing "We Want Emmon" buttons. People still stopped to talk to him everywhere he went. Women still gazed at him. He did not want any of them. He drifted off to sleep every night thinking about Laura, still feeling her warm breath on his arm.

How was it possible to be loved by so many people and still feel so alone? Death was not "the last enemy that will be abolished," as Emmon had heard the glum pastor recite from 1 Corinthians 15: 20-26 one Sunday at church.

Loneliness was.

7

Randy Yellowmander gazed at the layout for the next day's edition of *The Dunville Scooper*. The front-page story, of course, presented the latest ratings at the club. The Count had now been going on for seven months. Emmon won the January ratings, but Bill Dickens had been closing in on the lead more each month—he could very well overtake Emmon next month. He had started doing more of the observational humor Emmon specialized in, and his jokes reflected a sly wit Emmon lacked. Bill had watered down his pungent intellectual humor to a frothier brand the people of Dunville could more easily digest. As Randy looked over the front page of his paper, he silently wondered whether Bill had any more respect for his audience than Emmon did.

Marlon Grey fingered the trigger of the semi-automatic pistol, nervous waves pulsing through his body. Jittery excitement had been building for days, his nerve endings humming like fleas beneath his skin. Marlon had bought the pistol after his oldest son was born, but he had never used it or even picked it up since the day he brought it home and placed it in the top drawer of the desk in his den. He did not feel as satisfied as he thought he would now that he was actually holding it. Strange how life seemed more precious when you held the power to take it away. He was starting to have second thoughts for the first time since the action that seemed inevitable had first seeded in his brain. Marlon placed the pistol back in the top drawer of his desk and stared out at his dog lazing in the sun.

The race between Emmon and Bill was more heated than ever, causing that line of competition between the townsfolk to become even darker and deeper. Most of Bill's fans resided loyally in his camp, but some of them had lost respect for him for "pimping himself out to the common hicks" and refused to go to his acts anymore until he reclaimed his cerebral humor. Some of Emmon's fans defected to Bill's side as they came to believe more and more the gossip about Emmon's dubious efforts to both boost his image and eliminate his competition. Then there were the fans who clung like blind octopuses to Emmon's saintly, wholesome image, regardless of how many cleavers of reality came along to sever their arms of illusion. They believed in Emmon's good deeds, his inviting smiles, his warm handshakes. Emmon had inspired hope from the first time he took to the stage at The Dunville Jokebox. For his steadfast fans to abandon him now would mean losing that hope, and there was nothing worse in the world to lose than hope, especially for people who had once lost almost everything else.

Despite Laura's objections, her boss Russ insisted she schedule the acts so that Bill and Emmon performed back-to-back on the same night. A few of Emmon's fans would sometimes get to the club early, after Laura had taken the head count, so they could heckle Bill during his act, while a few of Bill's fans would pretend to leave and then reenter the club after the head count for Emmon's act so they could get in their fair share of heckling. Laura pleaded with Russ to prohibit heckling during acts, but he derived immense pleasure from the practice and even hoped for the heckling to mushroom into a good old-fashioned brawl. It would not take long for Randy Yellowmander to smell the blood; all people were just prey to him to be chewed up and spit back out on the pages of *The Scooper*. And any publicity was good publicity in Russ's mind.

One Friday night in the middle of February, one of Emmon's most adoring disciples, Freddy Flagstaff, got to the club a little before Emmon was set to go on and sat down at a table after most of Bill's audience had already broken up and scattered. He looked at the middle-aged man still sitting at the table, dressed in crisp tan slacks and a muted checkered sweater. Freddy surmised he was one of those professional types who resided in Dunville, probably because his wife preferred small-town life, but commuted into Boston for work every day.

"Damn, it's getting late. Better get to bed early; I can never sleep on the T," the middle-aged man uttered as he glanced at his watch, confirming Freddy's unspoken conjecture.

Freddy smirked. "Going to come back in after the head count and do some heckling during Emmon's act?"

The older man, Peter, countered with his own smirk. "Nah, that's for kids your age, who don't have anything better to do."

Freddy smarted; his smirk vanished. "What does that mean?"

Peter gave Freddy a patronizing smile, glossed with a thin coat of pity. "I've just overheard you talking to folks in here some nights. About how you just finished college and can't find a job, so you moved back in with your folks."

Freddy bristled, flames of anger kindling in his chest. Even among males in his younger, more "enlightened" generation, there was no sorer spot to rub than the inability to make money and provide, even if just for oneself.

"But don't worry about it, kid; something will come along eventually. In the meantime, keep comin' to Emmon's shows. I'm sure he makes you moochers feel better about yourselves; I hear he dropped out of college."

Blind rage seized Freddy. He grabbed the older man by the collar, bunching up his sleek cashmere wool sweater in his sweaty hand, now clenched in an iron fist. Peter had the advantage of working out at a state-of-the-art gym in Boston twice a week; he braced Freddy's wrists, wrenched his hand from his sweater, and threw him down to the floor. The bystanders were a mix of Emmon's fans and Bill's fans and seemed caught in the emotional crosshairs of fear and exhilaration. Peter looked down at Freddy, gave one last smirk, grabbed his jacket, and sauntered out the door, humming and fixing his disheveled sweater as he went.

Freddy sat against the outside wall of the club, his palms pressed against his heated, sweaty forehead. He had been brimming with optimism when he started college over six years ago, eager to fulfill his lifelong dream of becoming an architect. Constructing buildings and towers from Legos had come as naturally to him as throwing a ball. His friends had posters of baseball and basketball stars on their walls; his walls were adorned with pictures of buildings designed by Frank Lloyd Wright and Maya Lin. His friends read *Sports Illustrated*; he read *Architectural Digest*.

Freddy excelled in his studies at Northeastern University. He had expected to bask in a multitude of job offers upon graduating, but the fury of the recession obliterated even entry-level architectural jobs. He was all too happy to oblige when his parents asked him to move back home and help take care of his father, who had suffered a stroke that forced him to relearn even the most basic tasks. His father and the economy both started to recover after more than a year of paralyzing fear and despair, but Freddy could still find only a part-time job at a small architectural firm in Boston. He spent the rest of his week taking care of his father, reading, and looking for a full-time job. He would wake up in the middle of the night in his old childhood bed shivering with cold sweat, his heart hammering his chest with the dull gravity of a judge's gavel. What if he never found a full-time job? What if he never had the chance to become an esteemed architect? It was the greatest dream of his entire life, practically his reason for living. Now that the dream was slipping away, was there still a reason to live?

One night Freddy decided to check out the comedian at The Jokebox everyone was talking about. He was chugging his beer when Emmon Mims pranced onto the stage. Freddy felt an immediate connection to this young comedian who joked about student loans and unemployment. Emmon had a folksy manner and natural charm that enchanted the audience even more than the jokes themselves. From that point on, Freddy went to the club almost every week to see Emmon perform, and he made sure he was always in the audience for all of Emmon's acts once The Count started last July. Three nights a week for the past seven months, Freddy's feelings of fear, failure and worthlessness dissolved in a hot room brimming with joy and laughter.

Now tonight a stranger had wounded not only his wrists but also his pride, his humiliation stinging even worse than his burn marks. He did not want to go home; he did not want his parents to know how much he was hurting. He hated sleeping in the same bed he had slept in as a child and teenage boy; no matter how tightly he pulled the sheets around him, it was never enough to snuff out his shame and embarrassment. So Freddy Flagstaff sat outside The Dunville Jokebox and cried for a long time. And for the first time in over seven months, he had missed Emmon Mims's act.

8

The headline screeched with hawkish deadline: "Dickens Topples Mims in February Ratings."

There is no limit to the triumph that erupts when an underdog rises up and claims victory. Bill Dickens was the new town hero. Women who had adored Emmon from the beginning took down his picture and put Bill's in its place. The mayor invited him to dinner. And lest anyone suspect where his loyalties truly lie—he was not completely sure himself these days—Randy Yellowmander published an article syrupy enough to drown twenty pancakes about how Bill Dickens never forgot where he came from and how much he loved his hometown.

Bill Dickens hated his hometown. Mundrake was one of the oldest suburbs skirting Boston, and it seemed determined to remain firmly planted in the 1900s, keeping the twenty-first century at bay with the rough, calloused hands that labored in the small manufacturing plants checkering the town.

Men's collars were blue right down to their necks; most had gone to work in the plants right after high school, hard labor being the only kind of labor they valued. Girls had until their junior year to pick out a future husband before their mothers and grandmothers warned them of the dire prospect of becoming "old maids." Once married, couples had an average of three kids, two dogs and a cat—as long as it got along well with the dogs, of course. Men went off to work at the plants every morning. Women stayed home and packed lunches for their husbands and children, caught up on housework and errands, and then usually took a nap before getting dinner ready. Families huddled around the television after dinner every evening. The only thing more important than family in Mundrake was God. Most townsfolk attended Mundrake Methodist Church, the emotional gyroscope of the town. There were usually only three topics discussed at Sunday dinners: who was born, who died, and who got married.

A root of intellectualism began to grow strong in Bill in the midst of the commonality that flourished around him. He felt as though he had been born in a quotidian vortex, the nadir of suburban blandness. He was already reading at a fourth-grade level by the time he started school. He soon began a disciplined climb to scale the walls that separated Mundrake from the sophisticated, cosmopolitan world; he wanted to fly to the sun of the cultivated world. Bill begged his parents to send him to one of the esteemed private schools in Boston, but the tuition reached beyond their working-class incomes. He took the most advanced classes at the public school, which was not saying much, given the school's high dropout rate and poor national test scores. He read Shakespeare and Plato in his free time. He sent away for college brochures after he had discovered only a handful of brochures, all of them tattered and marred by missing pages, in the guidance counselor's office at school. Bill graduated at the top of his class and had been accepted to all of the universities to which he had applied—even Cornell, his "reach" school. He packed his bags three weeks before he was scheduled to move; he said goodbye to no one but his parents and younger brother.

Bill reveled in the company of the young intellectual elite when he first set foot on the Cornell campus. As the semester wore on, however, Bill could not seem to shake the feeling that he was wearing a tacky Halloween costume at an elegant ball. No matter how hard he tried, he just could not scrub away the stench of mediocrity. He transferred to Northeastern University, majoring in English and philosophy, but was not yet certain about what kind of career would scratch his intellectual itch. Then one day while tooling around on YouTube, Bill found a video of George Carlin performing his stand-up act, and a light switch turned on in his brain. Carlin joked about politics, philosophy and religion, and his audience was enthralled. Bill had found his intellectual hero and soon set his sights on following in his cerebral wake. He performed in a few strip clubs in Boston after graduating from Northeastern, but the audiences at those clubs failed to appreciate his intellectual humor. He heard about the comedy club started by Charles McVay in Dunville, and he knew some professional types planted themselves in some of the close Boston suburbs, including Dunville. Instead of trying to make it big in Boston right away, he would first gain traction on the inroads into the big city.

Bill arrived in Dunville a few weeks after Emmon. He did not cause the same volcanic eruption of excitement Emmon had, but he did appeal to the professional men and women in town, just as he had predicted, and eventually to the smartest students at the high school. Bill was aware that Emmon drew a bigger crowd, but he did not care so long as the townspeople considered him the "smart comedian." Then The Count began, and the number of people in the audience became more important than the type of people making up the audience, and Bill repeatedly came in second after Emmon, month after month. Nobody likes being second best, no matter how smart he is. As The Count went on, Bill softened his act, which he knew was just a less cynical way of saying he had dumbed down his act for the majority of people in Dunville who had never understood his cerebral humor laced with political, philosophical and religious references completely alien to them. Bill retained his clever wit but focused his act on more observational humor centered on suburban life and everyday human interactions. He closed in on Emmon more and more each month, due in equal measure to softening his act and to some of Emmon's fans believing the snowballing rumors about his dubious tactics to retain his lead in the contest.

Bill had always been confident he could win on his talent alone, but the pressures of competition slowly numbed his conscience, and he decided to put the discovery of Laura's abortion to good use by trying to blackmail Emmon into dropping out of the race. He had made a gross miscalculation, however, in thinking that Emmon's love for Laura had somehow softened his steely ambition, in believing the old axiom that "love conquers all." When Emmon refused to drop out of the competition, Bill made good on his threat to make Laura's abortion public news. Emmon retained his saintly status with the blind fans who remained loyal to him, however; it was Laura who was enduring most of the public humiliation. Soon Emmon and Bill were in a dead heat, and now Bill had finally dethroned Emmon. His victory was only by a small margin, but winning and losing only came in black or white packaging; victory knows no shades of grey. Bill was on top now. He had sold a part of his soul to get here—he knew it. Numbers and ratings, however, were more important than souls in Dunville these days.

No anger burned hotter than that of winners who have become losers. Emmon's fans bristled as they read the headline proclaiming Bill's victory in *The Scooper*. It was just not fair. Emmon was supposed to win. The town had loved him. He had lifted people out of despair. People were not supposed to turn their backs on a hero. And if Emmon's fans had always supported a man who was now a loser, did that mean they were now losers, too?

Anna Burrows grimaced at the numbers glaring from her alarm clock as the "beeps" blared with their usual cruel monotony. There had been a time when Anna did not even need an alarm to wake her up; she usually awoke as the sunlight tinged the room, bathing the furniture and television in a mustard haze. She had loved going to work every day and teaching the students about their nation's history, trying her best to bring historical characters and situations to life. Despite being embroiled in the usual dramas of adolescence, the students had loved their school and each other. Since The Count had begun, however, Anna dreaded going to work; every morning she asked herself how much longer she could stand to watch students taunt each other, fights break out in the hallways, friendships break apart. Then on the day following the release of the February ratings, Anna had to endure endless jeers from Bill's fans directed at Emmon's fans in the way of "Who are the fucking losers now?" Most of the Honors students still supported Bill, even after he had abdicated his intellectual humor in favor of softer "bubble gum" humor. They now took full advantage of the opportunity to crow about his victory in front of Emmon's fans. How could simple numbers, added up at the end of the month, be so powerful? Anna did not know the answer, as she was not a math teacher, but the question was keeping her up night after night.

Laura scanned the menu, trying hard to ignore the scornful stares of the other diners in Don's Deli Delights. Almost two months had passed since the form with her signature consenting to an abortion was revealed for all of Dunville to see, but the good townspeople had not yet found it in their hearts to forgive or forget. Laura never imagined forgiveness would be so hard to come by in a town that loved God so much. It was not, however, the same town in which she had arrived over a year ago, when the town was falling in love with Emmon. When she was falling in love with Emmon. Everything seemed simpler then. People were kind and loving, even as they were standing in the ruins of a massive economic earthquake. The people of Dunville were starting to pick up the broken pieces of their lives and glue the shards of joy and happiness back together again. Then The Count started, shattering the fragile dome of peace and tranquility the townsfolk had started to rebuild over their beloved little suburb. People were not so kind anymore. The town mantra soon became "Mims or Dickens," and you had to be on one side or the other. Then Emmon started to change, too. Laura knew he loved being the golden son, the savior of a dying town, but after The Count began, it was not enough just to be a savior—Emmon now had to be the *only* savior for the town, which, as Laura would later learn, meant others would have to be crucified.

Laura lassoed her dark memories, herded them to the back of her mind, and turned her attention back to the menu. A chicken salad sandwich and cold root beer always made everything better.

9

Mack McGraw was tired of losing. It seemed to have become the stock ending of every chapter of his life. It did not start out this way. He was born in Brookeville, one of the most idyllic suburbs lacing Boston. He liked school, earning mostly As and Bs in his courses. He grew up watching *My Three Sons* and *The Adventures of Ozzie and Harriet*, and he longed for the day when he would have his own children to tuck in at night, mostly good-natured children who occasionally needed some gentle guidance and gleaming pearls of paternal wisdom. First, though, he had to go to college—the next logical step on the path that would eventually lead right up to the white picket fence surrounding the quaint ranch-style house he would one day buy.

Mack had been accepted to three of the universities to which he had applied and ultimately decided on the University of Massachusetts Boston. About a week after his college acceptance letter came, his mother stood at the front door with a queer expression on her face; it reminded Mack of the look on her face whenever she was about to slip a lobster into boiling water. She gave him the envelope she had just fetched from the mailbox outside. Mack was not the smartest kid in school, but he knew immediately what it was—a draft notice. He tore it open but could not manage to read beyond the cheery "Greetings" salutation at the top of the letter. Some of Mack's high school friends had been drafted, but week after week slipped by, and no draft notice ever came. Until one day it did. Mack considered applying for a deferment, but one night he overheard his father and some neighborhood guys talking about how some "wusses" were "running off shitless" to Canada and how his father "would rather be shot dead than see Mack turn his back on his country." If a man was not old enough for people to mock his inability to turn a nice dollar, questioning his patriotism was the second-best emotional jab.

Mack went to the war. He completed two tours of duty, though he was never sure exactly what he was fighting. And after he had finished fighting, his country did not thank him. He stepped off the plane into a sea of protesters chanting "baby killer" and "rapist." All Mack wanted was to get on with a normal life, but the days of *Ozzie and Harriet* seemed a dozen lifetimes ago. He did not know where he belonged now. He did not want to stay in Brookeville; he felt like some displaced alien intruding on a peaceful colony of carefree earthlings. Shrapnel had shattered his knee, but that pain was nothing compared to his shattered mind. People Mack had known all his life would stare at him as they walked past, none of them ever stopping to ask how he was doing. They had condemned the "wusses" who had refused to go to war, but now that it was over, they did not want to be bothered with any of the casualties of that war. They loved their country. They believed people should die for their country—just as long as they did not have to see the carnage.

Mack eventually slipped into the suburban pocket of Dunville. The people seemed nice enough, and the town was teeming with small businesses and mom-and-pop stores. Mack had always pictured himself becoming an accountant or a teacher prior to the war. He enrolled in some classes at the University of Massachusetts Boston once he was settled in Dunville, but he just could not seem to slide neatly into college after the war. Every minute Mack sat in the classroom, he kept his eyes fixed on the hands of the student next to him, convinced his neighbor was going to pull out a gun any minute and put a bullet between his eyes. The numbers Mack worked with in his accounting class had no real meaning to him after he had watched men lose arms and legs and children get shot in the head. He just could not plug back into the world; it was not the world he had left behind when he went to war. Mack dropped out of college after two semesters and started a small lawn care business in Dunville. He would set his own hours and answer to nobody but himself. He never intended to answer to anyone again.

Mack's business ran smoothly. He did not like to be around people much—watching countless people die in front of him had dulled his affection for living, breathing people—but he enjoyed small talk with customers, and he had enough work to keep him busy and put food on the table. He still woke up in a cold sweat most nights, his hands clenching the bedspread, trying desperately to piece together the fragmented memories that lie scattered like a broken puzzle in his mind. Nevertheless, there was a cozy camaraderie in Dunville that made him feel warm and safe, and he could get through most days.

Then the recession blindsided the town as violently as the monsoons had razed villages in Vietnam, and having a pristine lawn was no longer a priority for people who did not know how they were going to feed their children some weeks. Mack's business folded. He forced himself to swallow his pride and dignity and apply for food stamps; it would have been easier to pour a bucket of rocks down his throat. The back of Mack's neck burned every time he pulled out his EBT card at the supermarket; he refused to look the cashier in the eyes. He prayed the other people in line could not see he was using an EBT card. One aimless day rolled after another; emails sent to prospective employers languished somewhere in cyberspace. Mack did not feel such shame and hopelessness since he had returned from the war.

One night Mack felt the walls of his small Cape Cod house close in so tightly he could barely breathe; being around people only rankled his nerves even more, but he wanted to go check out the new comedian in town. From the minute Emmon Mims ended his first joke, Mack felt his spirits lift. Emmon had an unfettered enthusiasm and buoyant charm that reminded Mack of himself when he was younger. Before he had killed in war. Before his country had turned his back on him. Before he had failed in business. Mack hitched his battered wagon to Emmon Mims's star, and he actually started going to bed happy at night. And once The Count began and Emmon won month after month, Mack was no longer just a happy fan—he was a happy *winner*. He had lost in war. He had lost his business. But now he supported this comedian who won in the ratings month after month. If Mack could never feel like a winner himself, he could at least bask in the reflected glory of a winner.

Now the basking was over. The headline announcing Bill Dickens's victory seemed to walk right off the page and wrap itself around Mack's throat. Then came the needling from Bill's fans; Bill now "ruled" and Emmon was a "loser." Shame and humiliation had bared their sharp, stained teeth again, but Mack refused to cower in their presence. He continued to go to Emmon's acts. He would not abandon his hero; Mack knew that kind of pain all too well.

Marlon Grey tried to block out his children's gleeful squeals of delight that intermittently escaped from the living room, where they were engrossed in an intense game of Operation. Misgivings still occasionally flitted like tiny black butterflies across his conscience, but he had regained his resolve to do what must be done. He had to do it. Marlon cast his eyes on the drawer that held the semi-automatic pistol; he had not looked at it in weeks. He shifted his gaze to the baby bluebirds in the tree outside his window, demanding their lunch from their mother with whiny squawks. Mack's son Joey bleated with puerile disappointment in the next room as the red nose of the flat cardboard patient lit up during his attempt to extricate the funny bone from the metal-edged cavity. Joey threw down the tweezers and glared at his older sister as she admonished him to go more slowly when removing the miniature plastic bones and innards. "The body is not just some piece of meat to cut into," Marlon overheard Peggy reprimand. He shivered slightly as he continued to gape at the tiny grumbling bluebirds.

Emmon was trying to stay in his apartment as much as possible since the release of the February ratings last week. He just could not face the people who no longer loved him. He knew that Bill had won by only fifty-two counts, but hairs of shame were easy to split. Emmon had arrived in Dunville over a year ago and helped free the townspeople from the tendrils of despair and hopelessness. Some now believed, however, that they had paid their debt to Emmon and abandoned him in favor of a smarter and wittier comedian who they also believed stood on firmer moral ground. Bill had even been kind enough to dumb down his act for the townsfolk, a favor that did not seem to offend them in the slightest. The shame and humiliation Emmon had buried in his hometown had resurfaced, trying with all their might to drag down his pride and dignity to the darkest depths of his soul. And the memory of seeing Laura's secret so callously exposed and the inescapable actuality of watching her suffer the unremitting public scrutiny exponentially amplified his own pain. He knew it was Bill who had broken into Laura's apartment and posted the signed consent form, but he also knew there was no evidence to prove it, knowledge that only fermented his acidic rage.

Nevertheless, Emmon would press on, just as he always had. Just as he had watched Laura do in the preceding months. Once the survivor in you was born, there was no quieting its resolve.

10

Laura sat at her desk reading the latest letter from her sister Lana. As with her last three letters, Lana again expressed how sorry she was that Laura had lost the baby. She had come for a surprise visit almost a month after Laura had found out she was pregnant, and Laura just had to talk with someone about the doubts she was feeling. Lana had insisted Laura's feelings would pass "in no time at all," accentuating this opinion with a sweet smile and a snap of the fingers. After promising not to tell anyone, Lana had returned to their hometown, where she still resided, and promptly told everyone in the family. They would notice soon enough, anyway, right? A few weeks later, Laura broke the news that she had lost the baby, which was close enough to the truth without being the entire truth. Since then, at least one female member of Laura's family called her every week or, in Lana's case, wrote her a heartfelt letter every few weeks. Laura looked at the postmark on the envelope. She always laughed to herself whenever she thought about the name of her hometown: *Hope Meadows.*

More like a pit of despair. Located in southeastern Massachusetts, Hope Meadows was one of the smallest towns in the state. There were approximately five hundred residents when Laura was born, but the population had grown to a whopping twelve hundred by the time she left for college. There were a total of four traffic lights in town. Laura had to ride her bike five miles to the next town to read a book, as the residents of Hope Meadows apparently saw no need for a library.

Her mother and father had been high school sweethearts and married three weeks after graduation. Her mother, Lynette, had been a whiz at math, but she had had no plans to continue her education beyond the high school classroom. Her father went on to study engineering at Wentworth Institute of Technology and began his career in an entry-level position at an esteemed engineering firm in New Bedford. They vowed to stay in their hometown forever, but even in a small rural town like Hope Meadows, with its low cost of living, they struggled to pay the mortgage and buy food every month, so Lynette put her algorithmic flair to use and took some accounting classes at the nearby community college in order to buoy her fledgling household. She landed a part-time accounting job at a small law firm in Fall River. Laura's father was ascending the career ladder at his firm, and Lynette became pregnant with Laura four years after she had started her job. She had been promoted to a higher position a few months before she became pregnant, and she toyed with the idea of going back to work after Laura was born when her own mother eagerly offered to take care of the baby during the day. Lynette's girlfriends and older sisters were mortified when she told them of her plans and lectured Lynette about the precious moments and fleeting joys of childhood a mother must not miss. Nobody lectured Laura's father on having to be there for those ephemeral moments and joys.

Lynette quit her job and soon joined her friends for play dates and Mommy and Me classes, which she would continue for ten more years as Laura was joined by two sisters and a brother. Laura's most indelible memory from her childhood was watching her mother trying to quiet a screaming infant with food stains around its mouth, who was taking great delight in creaming the untouched food on the small plastic tray with a brightly colored plastic spoon. Laura vowed to herself that she would never be in the same position as her mother. She stuck to her studies with unyielding dedication and cried tears of joy (or was it relief?) when she was accepted to Boston University.

Starting college felt like being launched into a new galaxy, a scholastic Milky Way containing a solar system in which stately buildings, expansive lecture halls, and esteemed professors orbited around one bright, shining goal—achievement. Her enthusiasm was deflated during her phone conversation with her mother after her first full week of classes, and the first question her mother asked pertained not to classes, new friends or activities but to Laura's prospects for dating and mating, an inquiry she would reiterate over the next four years, even as Laura's phone calls to home became less and less frequent. Her mother's persistent calls henpecking about her dating life punctured Laura's sheer enthusiasm for college like a needle through a balloon.

Laura majored in human resources management and happily balanced her classes with track and student government. She dated occasionally, but her studies, friends and campus activities absorbed most of her energies. She graduated right into the gaping mouth of the national recession, but she managed to keep it from swallowing her career ambitions. Laura searched fruitlessly for a job for five months, then one of her girlfriends from college called and told her about the new comedy club recently established in Dunville. Laura figured she had to start somewhere, and Russ Manning hired her as his assistant manager on the spot.

Laura had not planned on falling in love; that joy was scheduled for much later in her lifetime planner, after she had firmly established herself in her career and needed only pure, unadulterated love, not economic sustenance, from a relationship. Then she saw Emmon Mims, and a strange, tingly feeling kindled in her chest. Laura rarely watched the comedians perform their acts, but she always stood next to the window at the front of the club when Emmon was performing. She wondered now if Emmon ever knew that. She did not actually talk to him until she ran into him one night in the club kitchen. Laura pretended to be taken aback when she saw him, but in truth, she had seen him walk past her office, presumed he was going to the kitchen, and decided to follow him. Soon they were running into each other in the kitchen at least once a week. One afternoon, Emmon asked her to drive with him out to the pond. They were soon going out to the pond, the beach or the park every week. It did not matter whether they were basking in the sun or goggling at the crystalline stars; Laura felt like she had slipped into a warm bath whenever she was lying next to Emmon.

Her happiness was dimmed by the rumors quietly floating around the club like cigar smoke in a sitting room. Some believed that Emmon was conspiring with Randy Yellowmander to buff and shine his image and ensure his victory in The Count after Yellowmander had published three stories over the course of four weeks detailing how kindhearted Emmon Mims had come to the aid of a stranded motorist, with each story accompanied by a picture to show Emmon's kindheartedness in action. It was rare, after all, to see a stranded motorist by the side of the road in Dunville except during the harsh winter months, and Emmon had managed to come upon three in the benign fall weather. One of the other comedians at the club, Eddie Neymeyer, half-jokingly stated that "God makes a car break down whenever Emmon is around—and always throws in a bystander to take a picture." Laura swatted the rumors away like annoying flies at first. Emmon did love publicity, but he would never stoop to the level of staging opportunities for himself to play the hero—would he?

Then Yellowmander published the article on Phil Rigley's past indecent exposure conviction. Laura just could not believe that Emmon had anything to do with getting the story published. Emmon was ambitious, but he would never actually cross the line into sleaze territory—would he?

Laura learned she was pregnant about a week after the article on Phil Rigley came out in *The Scooper*. She felt a strange detachment after her doctor gleefully told her the news, as though she was watching a scene from a movie. She was not really there, in her doctor's office, listening to him tell her she was pregnant. Laura had been to her cousins' gender reveal parties and baby showers and patiently held her tongue when one of her aunts assured her in a patronizing tone that she would eventually change her mind about wanting a baby. Images of her harried mother toiling over screaming kids, breaking up sibling squabbles, and later, hustling the children from one extracurricular activity to another played in Laura's mind like an interminable slideshow.

Laura loved her mother and appreciated the sacrifices she had made for her children, but now that she was an adult, Laura had no real sense of who her mother was as a person. She did not know what her mother cared about, what interests or passions stoked her beyond yearning for grandchildren. She felt like she knew her father even less, beyond the fact that he was a very successful engineer who had provided handsomely for his family; they seemed to have little to talk about when Laura came home for a visit.

Laura's unofficial title in town was "Emmon Mims's Girlfriend." Emmon's fans barely even acknowledged her when they came up to talk to him. When she was out and about town by herself, women would come up to her to ask about Emmon. Was Emmon funny when he was not on stage? When did she realize he was "The One"? Were they going to get married soon? After the baby was born, her title would become "Mother of Emmon Mims's Child." As much as that thought made Laura squirm, she still could not decide whether to go through with an abortion. She was stuck at the mental crossroads where pride and self-preservation had come face-to-face with her conscience and compassion.

Laura remained stuck in her muddy indecision until the beginning of December. She had a migraine and decided to take a nap in the utility room in the basement; sleeping on the worn mattress was at least better than sitting at her desk with a stack of papers piled in front of her. Laura rarely went downstairs during the day, as she had so much work to do, but she desperately needed a break from the fluorescent lights in her office, and the door to the basement was just across from her office. She was halfway down the stairs when she heard Emmon railing at someone in the dark basement.

"Don't give me that, Yellowmander! Don't tell me there's nothing we can use."

A few seconds of silence. Then Laura got it; Emmon was talking to Randy Yellowmander on his phone.

"Dickens *has* to have a skeleton in his closet. And if he doesn't have a skeleton, then at least a few bones we can make *into* a skeleton."

More silence. Laura started to feel queasy, and she knew it was not because of the baby.

"Yeah, yeah, I know. But look, if we can get rid of a nice kid like Phil Rigley, then we can surely dispose of a pretentious douchebag like Bill Dickens," Emmon said in a calmer voice.

Laura slumped against the stair railing, tears pooling in her eyes. The slap of reality stings so hard. She had done her best to hold the rumors back from her luminous circle of love and happiness, but the truth always floods over any dam built by denial. Now she knew the truth; it was not just sweet, sentimental stories and pictures Emmon and Randy Yellowmander were planting in *The Scooper*—Emmon was burning people in his scalding, white-hot determination to win. And Emmon might very well win The Count, but he had to pay for his sins, for the pain he had caused. He had won the hearts of Dunville residents. He had won the ratings month after month. But Laura now had the power to take something from Emmon that Randy Yellowmander could not help him to ever win back. Laura's anger and disillusionment became glued to the feelings of pride and self-preservation that had been wrestling with her conscience for the past two months, forming a messy but firm mental resolve to do something her family had always believed was the vilest sin a woman could ever commit. The next day Laura started researching abortion clinics in Massachusetts.

Now Laura sat at her desk holding yet another letter from her sister Lana expressing how sorry she was that Laura had lost the baby. She folded the letter, placed it back in the envelope, and threw it in the trash. She looked at the clock. It was late. Time to go home, go to bed, and start again in the morning.

11

Randy Yellowmander learned early the power of words and pictures. He had grown up in Brighton, a quiet suburb neighboring Dunville. Randy served as editor of the school newspaper in high school, and his classmate Bennie Buckley decided to run for class president during their sophomore year. Two weeks before the election, Randy was walking to the gym to get a picture of the new bleachers when he saw Bennie talking to Frank Sullivan, a student who had been paralyzed in a car accident the year before. Bennie noticed Randy and asked him to snap a picture of him and Frank together. Randy obliged and then wrote an article in the school newspaper highlighting Bennie's respect and compassion for his fellow students. Bennie won the election for class president by a large margin. Randy was not sure if the photo op and article were solely responsible for Bennie's victory, but he was convinced it had some effect. Forget pulling a rabbit out of a hat or sawing a woman in half—words and pictures were magic in black and white. It did not matter whether William Randolph Hearst ever actually made the statement "You furnish the pictures and I'll furnish the war"—it would become Randy's mantra in the cutthroat world of journalism.

Randy's most ardent desire after graduating from Suffolk University was to run his own newspaper; it would, after all, be difficult to furnish a war if he was not in charge. However, he could not start out being the chief editor for *The New York Times*. He had to start a little lower than that, so when his father told him that his friend Bob McNally was retiring as editor for *The Dunville Scooper*, Randy quickly volunteered for the position.

His primary goal was to increase circulation. Fear and violence had always sold newspapers, but they were hard to come by in the placid suburb of Dunville and its three neighboring suburbs—Brighton, Newton and Fairberry—*The Scooper* also covered. Randy mostly filled the pages of his newspaper with articles detailing pedestrian suburban events such as bake-offs, high school sports games, and school plays, always being certain to highlight any fights, conflicts or dramatic scenes that had occurred at these events. Randy still glowed with pride whenever he thought about the picture he published of Gladys Roundtree staring pathetically at the chili pot she had just thrown down in an indignant rage after Florence Sommersby had been declared the winner of the 10th Annual Great Chili Cook-Off.

Once the recession hit, *The Scooper*'s circulation nosedived even further. Randy started featuring heart-wrenching stories of residents who had lost their homes and struggled to buy groceries every week, and circulation boosted slightly; people were never too broke to see their own misery in print. After The Jokebox opened in July 2009, Randy published an article every few weeks profiling one of the comedians at the club. And when Emmon Mims became the town's beloved son later that year, Randy featured a glowing two-page spread on the young comedian. There was no need to glorify Emmon beyond that, however; nothing was at stake then. Then Jada McKinna's kidnapping the spring after Emmon had arrived at the club provided plenty of sensational grist for Randy's paper mill.

Then The Count began the next July, and Emmon was no longer just a beloved comedian; he was now a competitor. If Randy could not furnish a war, he could at least stoke one. He wanted Emmon to win; he needed some of his prize money so he could escape Dunville and get his feet planted in New York. When he first formed his alliance with Emmon last September, Randy would have one of his photographers follow Emmon around town and snap heartwarming pictures of the beloved comedian with his arm around a devoted fan—or even better, an adorable child. A real man of the people. Randy's photographer was also at Boston's Children Hospital when Emmon paid a visit and posed with several of the children in their hospital beds. If there was one thing more heartwarming than posing with an adorable child, it was posing with an adorable *sick* child. Jada McKinna quickly disappeared from the headlines.

Randy soon got craftier with the photo ops. Anyone could pose with a fan, but how many local celebrities would take the time to stop and help someone stranded on the side of the road? Randy threw in a few pictures of Emmon doing just that in late September and early October. The fact that Emmon had tinkered with the person's car in the early morning hours and then later followed the said car with Randy lying in the backseat, ready to snap a picture, was just a pesky little detail that did not need to be included.

Apparently not all Dunville residents were as naive and tenderhearted as Randy and Emmon had presumed, however. Some of Emmon's fans started to desert him, dismissing him as a complete phony. Nevertheless, many stayed loyal to him; they just could not desert a man who had made them feel happy and alive again. In their minds, Emmon was a hero. And once a hero, always a hero.

The biggest test of loyalty for Emmon's fans came when the article revealing Phil Rigley's past sex crime conviction was revealed in *The Scooper*. Emmon remembered that Phil had once started to say something about how Cranston, Rhode Island was a great place to grow up but then abruptly changed the subject. He also remembered that Phil had told people he had been born and raised in Providence when he had first arrived in Dunville. Emmon also knew Phil was moving up in the ratings—and any threat was a big threat when you were on top. Randy eagerly went on his sleaze expedition and eventually unearthed Phil's past arrest and conviction. He knew what Phil's defense had been and even believed it, but he did not include it in the article he published. He knew it was over for Phil the minute people read "indecent exposure to minors." Even if they were not sure if the charges of which Phil had been convicted were true or suspected there was more to the story, accusations presented in block letters on the front page of the local newspaper spewed bitter venom. Phil Rigley left Dunville. But some of the venom had hit Emmon, too; some of his fans, disgusted as they were with Phil, could not help but wonder if Emmon had given Randy a little nudge toward digging in Phil's past dirt. Many of Emmon's fans, however, kept his sins and misdeeds hidden safely away in their blind spots.

It pained Randy to publish the headline announcing Bill's victory over Emmon in the February ratings, not because he empathized with Emmon's humiliation over being dethroned, but because he had devoted months to propping up a man who was now in second place. No victory for Emmon meant no money for Randy. He might forever be stuck in the small pond of Dunville when he longed to swim with the big fish in New York City. He could not get a leg up and keep it up in the big city without a nice cushion of cash under his feet, not with his crushing student loan debt. Worse still, Randy had just spoken with Laura; if this month's numbers continued on their current trajectory, Bill would win the March ratings by over three hundred counts—a much greater edge than he had achieved in February. Things were not looking good.

Emmon stepped out on stage and grabbed the microphone. He opened his mouth to start his usual friendly banter with the audience, but he suddenly froze like an electronic toy dog whose batteries had just died. Emmon had not been the same since Bill Dickens had overtaken him in the February ratings. And Randy Yellowmander had told him a few hours ago that Dickens had an even wider lead this month. Emmon was sliding down an emotional avalanche, battered by the unrelenting mental rocks of fear, loneliness and humiliation. He looked out at the audience; the crowd seemed like a bunch of smiling ghosts. Nothing around him seemed real, as if he was watching a movie from a dark corner of a small theater. His throat tightened. Beads of sweat dotted his forehead. The crowd was drawing further and further away; the room was getting darker. He was not going to make it. His knees felt weak. His head felt like a deflated basketball.

Then he saw her. She stood next to the window at the front of the club, the fading sunlight burning apricot streaks into her ginger hair. Her skin gleamed like rose-tinted porcelain. It was Laura. She gave Emmon a small but warm smile. She nodded her head slightly.

Emmon felt like he had just drunk the sweetest shot of whiskey on the planet. His legs steadied. The room was warm and bright again. He saw the people clearly in front of him now. He came alive and resurrected the old Emmon Mims, the shining young man with whom Dunville had fallen in love all those long months ago. Emmon breezed through his act with the zest of a zombie who had just been given back his soul.

12

The atmosphere was as tense as ever at Dunville High as April showed its bright, cheery face. Randy Yellowmander had included the overall tallies for each comedian in yesterday's article announcing March's ratings. Emmon was at 9,182; Bill Dickens, 7,433. All of the other comedians were riding the faint tails of Emmon's and Bill's comets. Jack Bailey, a rather stiff and awkward young man whose cohabitating arrangement with his parents provided most of the fodder for his jokes, came in a distant third place at 3,725. In the excitement of Dickens's triumph, everyone had forgotten the reality that was hiding in plain sight—Emmon's lead in the ratings for seven consecutive months. Bill would have to exceed Emmon by at least 1,749 head counts over the next three months in order to win The Count. A reach, but both Emmon and Bill knew it was possible, as did the kids at Dunville High.

Few students were more elated about Dickens's recent triumphs than Susan Brightman. Steered onto the "gifted" track after she had scored 140 on an IQ test in middle school, Susan was known as "the smartie" among the townsfolk. She had wanted to shuck "the common folk," as she affectionately referred to the teachers and students at Dunville High, and go to one of the elite private schools, but her parents' wallets were much smaller than Susan's brains and ambitions. She had thought some about going to a magnet school, but she had not yet narrowed down any of her myriad intellectual interests to one specific focus, one guiding star in the cerebral night sky. Susan therefore continued to attend Dunville High with the strained enthusiasm of a superb baseball player still consigned to the minor league, waiting to climb to hallowed higher ground. She was not especially popular with the other students, who occasionally gently teased her for being a "dork" and a "nerd"—being "the smartie" could be a lonely burden to bear. Susan's greatest enemies were the "it girls" who wore the latest fashions, idolized the Kardashians, and seemed intent on making a whole new school subject out of flirting with boys. Susan hated them, and they returned the animosity in equal measure, wrapped in the superficial, paper-thin nastiness used copiously in the world of teenage girls.

These braindead tarts, as Susan always referred to them, fell hard for Emmon Mims when he first came to town. Even the star quarterback at Dunville High began to pale in comparison to Emmon; he was hope and joy wrapped up in a beautiful, quaint package. He made little impression on Susan, however; his gleaming smile and folksy charm merely camouflaged his lack of wit and talent. Emmon Mims seemed as bland and lollipop as a clown at a child's birthday party, only much prettier and less frightening. None of the comedians, in fact, made any impression on Susan. Then Bill Dickens arrived in town, and Susan discovered her kindred intellectual spirit. She hated that he had pruned his cerebral humor to make it less dense for "the common folk," but his jokes were still smarter and wittier than Emmon's, and she was ecstatic when Bill trounced

Emmon in the February ratings. Susan felt proud to be smart for the first time in her life.

Susan leaned against the wall in the school corridor reading the top story in *The Scooper* highlighting Dickens's victory in the March ratings. She looked up and saw Tara Teasdale and Mindy Morrison, the reigning queens of the "it girls," glaring at her with piercing, catty eyes. Susan coolly flipped the paper over, abruptly throwing the headline announcing Dickens's triumph in the queen cats' faces. Tara's bright red lips contorted into a scathing frown.

"Your boy Dickens is Mr. Popular now because this town doesn't know the meaning of loyalty, but he's the same *loser* he's always been," Tara spat, every word drenched in thick venom.

"He is winning now because he changed his jokes to ones that the Neanderthals and tarts in this town could better understand. I doubt they even know the meaning of the word *sit*," Susan retorted. "And because everyone knows Mims would sell his mother to win this thing."

"Emmon is ten times the man Bill is. How many kids' hospitals has *Dickhead* visited?"

Susan smirked. "You don't have to go around kissing sick kids when you actually have brains and talent."

Tara bristled; she pulled her lips tight. "You goddam little snob. Someone needs to teach you a lesson—the kind you don't learn sitting in front of the fucking chalkboard."

Tara grabbed Susan's left arm and pinned it behind her back, while Mindy did the same with her right arm. They hoisted Susan off the ground and carried her through the side doors leading to the courtyard. Tara and Mindy seemed to be sharing the same mean teenage-girl brain that did not understand compassion or virtue. They looked at the holly shrub squatting in the margins of the courtyard and then looked at each other and smirked. This was going to be good. Susan blanched as she realized what was about to happen.

"No, please, *don't*," Susan pleaded, panic coursing through her every word.

"A calculator and mechanical pencil can't help you now, can they, you snotty bitch?" Tara snidely queried as she and Mindy plopped Susan down on the ground and began tearing off her clothes.

"Stop, please, *stooooop*," Susan beseeched in a pitifully tortured voice.

"You're so smart—figure a way out, genius," Mindy sneered as she ripped off Susan's underwear, the last of her garments.

Tara braced Susan's wrists while Mindy grabbed her ankles. They hoisted her up, swung her back and forth like a sack of potatoes, then tossed her into the holly shrub and ran.

No horror movie queen could have outdone Susan's shriek as she landed in the shrub, the spiny leaves cutting into her flesh like dozens of tiny razor blades. No part of her body was shielded from the serrated leaves; every inch of her flesh burned in fiery pain. Her howls followed one another in rapid succession, creating a ghastly, perverse melody everyone in the school could hear.

Teachers and students began to spill out of the school doors, tripping over each other, trying to pinpoint the exact location of those bloodcurdling howls. Peter Billings detected something violently shaking in the holly bush on the right side of the courtyard; he led the way as the crowd marched behind him. Peter discerned a naked form struggling in the bush; he and Mr. Landry, one of the math teachers, hoisted Susan out.

The crowd gaped as Susan stood naked in front of them, sobbing and shivering, despite the warm spring breezes. Short red slashes crisscrossed her fair skin from her forehead to her feet. Susan could feel everyone's stares burning into her as sharply as had those serrated leaves. Someone finally brought a blanket, wrapped it around Susan, and walked her to the nurse's office.

One of Randy Yellowmander's reporters managed to get a picture of Susan Brightman lying in her hospital bed checkered with gauze pads and wearing a forlorn expression. Perfect. This was the kind of picture that made Randy feel as giddy as a drunken meerkat. Good pictures tug at the heartstrings; the best ones wrench the nerves. People just could not resist getting a glimpse of suffering, despite all of their clucking and crying and moaning. Randy proudly inserted the picture of Susan in her hospital bed under the blaring headline "Girl Hurled into Bush at Dunville High, Suffers Serious Injuries."

If Randy Yellowmander were the kind of man to believe in an afterlife, he would have told himself that, somewhere, William Randolph Hearst was laughing.

Emmon forced himself to get out of bed and walk to the kitchen. He opened the cupboard and stared blankly at the various assortment of cereals. He grabbed one of the boxes and listlessly poured the cereal into a bowl. Emmon had been riding an emotional upswing the past few weeks, but he was hovering much closer to the ground now, his feet kicking around hopelessly in the debris of his wrecked life. There was barely an empty seat in the club on nights when Bill Dickens had performed this month; more than half of the seats sat naked during Emmon's performances. Fewer people stopped to talk to Emmon on the street or waited for him to arrive at the club these days. Randy Yellowmander still arranged occasional photo ops with Emmon's most devoted fans, but the days of swaying the masses with heartwarming pictures had long since passed. People yearn for colorful, sweet elixirs when they are wasting away, but those panaceas quickly lose their enchantment once people regain their health and vigor. Many people in town simply felt that Emmon had nothing more to give to them now that they were no longer teetering on an economic precipice.

Emmon dawdled over his cereal, trying in earnest to arrange the remaining Cheerios into the letter "L." He finally threw his spoon down in frustration after five failed attempts. He just could not do anything right anymore. Emmon thought about going back to bed, but he just could not bring himself to give up—that is what Bill Dickens had wanted since The Count began. So Emmon dragged himself into the shower, lingered under the hot water for twenty minutes, dried himself off, and then threw on a pair of jeans and a sweatshirt.

Sauntering down the street, Emmon noticed the luminous yellow tulips swaying alongside the sidewalk and the bluebirds fluttering around the cherry blossoms exploding like dazzling seashell pink fireworks. A satiny monarch butterfly landed gingerly on his arm and idled for a minute. He had never really appreciated any of these small wonders in all the time he had been in Dunville.

Emmon came upon the park he and Laura used to visit every couple of weeks. He watched as the carousel whirled in exuberant circles. A warm feeling spread over him like melted butter as he remembered the time he and Laura had stayed up all night talking on the lifeless carousel. He could still see Laura lying sideways on the back of the tawny mustang, its resplendent wooden beauty and frozen smile gleaming in the pearly moonlight. She had smiled as she christened her horse "Scotty" and then laughed as she noticed that her long ginger hair had become entangled with Scotty's chocolate mane.

Memories of his time with Laura always made Emmon feel sad, so he shifted his gaze to the scattering of people on the park grounds. A father and son were idly tossing a football back and forth. Emmon's vision blurred as his eyes puddled with tears. He would be holding his child in two more months, if Laura had not—

Emmon abruptly turned his thoughts off and scurried off to the club. It was his last performance before April was over.

13

The headline on the front page of *The Dunville Scooper* trumpeted another win for Bill Dickens. His tally for April was 1,190, with Emmon at 490. Emmon's total tally now came to 9,672; Bill, 8,623. If Emmon continued to slip, Bill could surpass Emmon in the total tally when The Count ended at the end of June. The ground was sliding out from under Emmon's feet, and Randy Yellowmander was feeling almost as unbalanced as Emmon these days.

Randy regained some of his emotional equilibrium in the second week of May after Susan Brightman finally recounted exactly how she had come to land in the holly shrub last month. Tara Teasdale and Mindy Morrison were now officially charged with assault. A teenage girl thrown into a bush and lacerated with serious cuts, and two other teenage girls going to court and possibly being expelled from school—a delectable story. Randy included in his article a statement from Tara and Mindy revealing that the fight had started because Susan had literally thrown Bill's March win in their faces. Maybe this incident would generate renewed interest in Emmon, who had some fans so devout and steadfast they mutilated one of Bill's fans. Randy could picture packs of townsfolk going to some of Emmon's shows just to see the man at the center of the savage drama. It was not exactly a plane crash or mass shooting, but for

Randy Yellowmander, chief editor of a small suburban newspaper, it was pretty damn close.

Laura reclined against the large oak tree mounted next to the pond like a grotesque, gnarly wooden statue. She had sat against this old oak on her first date with Emmon, while he had looked up at the sky, discerning animals among the bulging cloud puffs. Laura lifted her head, but there were no clouds in the sky, limpid as sapphire glass on this balmy day in the middle of May. The sun peered down on the lush grass shimmying to the silent beat of the warm, tender breezes. Perky dandelions turned their little yellow faces up to the sun.

Laura could not stand being cooped up in her office during her lunch hour. In fact, she was finding it harder and harder to be at the club at all these days. For a while, it seemed like Emmon had resurrected his ebullient charm, which seemed to have died a slow, tortured death since Bill Dickens had displaced him in the February ratings. For the past few weeks, however, a dark sheen had once again fallen over Emmon. He barely talked to anyone anymore, hardly ever even lifted his eyes from the ground. And since the April ratings had come out a couple of weeks ago, Emmon would arrive at the club just a few minutes before he was set to go on, scamper onto the stage, spit out his jokes, and then scurry backstage. He avoided looking at Laura when she was around.

Laura almost always came to either the park or the pond during her lunch break, and on this day, she sat watching the downy baby ducks trailing their sleek mother on the glossy surface of the pond, their tiny webbed feet peddling swiftly through the crystalline water. Laura wondered if Emmon was thinking about their child that would be arriving next month, if she had not gone through with the abortion. Had she done the right thing? Laura still felt no desire to become a mother, but she could not help feeling a little sad for Emmon, despite his sins. He had lost her, his child, and the love and admiration of many of his fans. He had set the stage for his own downfall with his dubious alliance with Randy Yellowmander, but "you are supposed to love your man unconditionally," Laura's mother and aunts had always sermonized. The worst men in history had women who loved them.

No. She would not stand quietly by Emmon's side and support him no matter what he did. Her love had conditions—honesty, integrity, honor, compassion. Emmon had violated those conditions, and he had to pay a price. To Laura's surprise, some of Emmon's fans were not freely giving out their love and support, either. They were not all as clueless as she had thought; some correctly surmised that Randy Yellowmander, sleazy as he was, would not have been motivated solely on his own to dig up some dirt on Phil Rigley. Some of Emmon's fans became more convinced than ever that Randy and Emmon were in murky cahoots after the story on Rigley had appeared in *The Scooper* and simply lost faith in their beloved comedian. Others started to appreciate Bill Dickens more once he thinned out his dense intellectual humor but continued to deliver his jokes in witty wrappings; Emmon's jokes started to sound lame and obvious by comparison.

Emmon once held the love of the people in his hand like a crystal orb; now it was slipping through his fingers like sludge. And he would never hold his child now, either. Laura's eyes blurred with tears as she watched the mother duck slice through the gossamer pondweed, her sprightly ducklings in tow.

83

Randy Yellowmander seemed to have 20/20 vision when it came to discerning human nature. There were not as many empty seats during Emmon's performances after Randy published the article revealing the whole story behind Susan Brightman's attack. The minority of Dunville residents who had never even been interested in The Count fluttered to the club like zealous moths entranced by the torrid flames of death and destruction. Two girls loved Emmon Mims so much they had thrown another girl into a bush. Just as people suddenly became interested in the movies of an actor ensnared in a scandal, people swarmed to the club to see the comedian who had spurred two girls to attack another. Emmon's numbers spiked. By the time May was over, Emmon had tallied 822; Bill, 1,200.

Emmon Mims was back from the dead, helped out of his grave by the slick hands of Randy Yellowmander.

14

The first day of June greeted the town of Dunville with the incandescent sun beaming in the unblemished azure sky. The townsfolk eagerly snatched up *The Dunville Scooper* to see the May ratings. Emmon's total tally was now 10,494; Bill Dickens had reached 9,823. This was the last month of The Count. The lurid renewed interest in Emmon had started to wane by the end of last month, but even if he tallied only 530 people in this last month and Bill netted a full 1,200, Emmon would win The Count. Bill had never believed in God; he always trusted that he could take care of himself. Nobody was an atheist when he was fighting for his life, however, and Bill suddenly started doing a lot of praying.

Bill and Emmon always made every effort to avoid each other. Emmon was about to leave the club after his act one night when he heard Bill talking with a couple of the other comedians.

"Where ya gonna go when you win the big money, Bill?" Dave Peters asked as he stretched an elastic band on his fingers.

"What difference does it make? We'll be brushing off his dust no matter where he goes," Gus Winfield gushed.

Bill smirked. "Don't worry; in another decade, you'll be reading about me under the latest 'Where Are They Now?' segment."

Beneath the cynicism oozing from him like bubbling larvae, Bill felt his heart cool into jagged volcanic rock. He never wanted to be forgotten and the world to move on without him—he would sooner die. But he knew that fame wore the flimsiest of coats. Just look at what had happened to Emmon; it seemed like not a week went by that Bill did not see a rusted "We Want Emmon" pin lying on the ground. Bill loved the attention, the glory of being the local celebrity, but the warm glow he felt when people smiled and stopped to talk to him always cooled a little when he remembered that Emmon had once been the town's golden boy. One minute, fame shone like a diamond; the next, it was as cold and obscure as a stone in the sand. Why did fame have to totter on gossamer hands and knees instead of walking on steel legs?

Bill shooed these ugly thoughts to the darkest part of his mind and laughed and joked with the other comedians late into the night.

Emmon walked down the street in buoyant strides. There were still plenty of empty seats on nights when he performed, but he could do math as well as Dickens. All he needed was five hundred thirty people, at the most, to come to his performances this last month of The Count. Then he would win the one hundred thousand dollars, give a quarter of it to Randy Yellowmander, and then dump this suburban pit. Emmon would find greener comic pastures; maybe try his luck on television. Other people would write smart jokes for him, and he would deliver them with his breezy charm. It was not over for him. He could . . . Emmon halted in his tracks. He backpedaled to the newsstand he had just ambled past. He looked down at the copy of *The Dunville Scooper* sitting atop a towering stack of fresh, smooth papers. He stared at the headline shouting in thick block letters: DUNVILLE HIGH STUDENT DIES FROM STAPH INFECTION.

Susan Brightman had developed a staph infection that had spread to her heart and died yesterday afternoon in the hospital. Emmon did not have to read the entire article to know that the staph infection had resulted from Susan's wounds suffered from being thrown into the bush and that at least one of her cuts or punctures had not been properly bandaged. Emmon looked up at the newspaper vendor, who barely caught Emmon's glance before swiftly looking away. Emmon did not know what to say; it was one of those rare moments he could not just fill with a lame joke. He turned away and walked back to his apartment. He unlocked his door and grabbed a beer from the fridge. He sat on the couch for a long time, soothing the queasy feeling in his stomach with one can of beer after another.

Emmon awoke just as the early morning light began to filter through the filmy teal curtains. He tried to sit up, but it felt like someone had plopped a bag of potatoes on his head. An acid feeling burned in his chest and slithered up into his throat. He buried his face in his pillow as images from the past year marched through his heavy head. Susan Brightman was dead. Tara Teasdale and Mindy Morrison had been charged with assault—and now an even worse charge. Phil Rigley was back in his hometown, his chance for success ruthlessly yanked out from underneath him. It did not take long for dirt from a sex crime involving minor children to spread and transmute to mud in the entertainment business; Phil would be lucky if the seedy strip clubs allowed him to perform. And Emmon's unborn child was gone.

Emmon knew he was the reason for all of this destruction. Through actions big and small, direct and indirect, he had dug the graves for these ruined lives. Emmon looked out the window, as if somewhere out there he could find some key to a time machine that would allow him to turn back the clock, back to that afternoon when Laura had sat by the pond and he had lain on his back looking up at the laughing dog cloud. He would live that day over again twenty times if he could. And Laura would still be lying next to him every night if he had the power to change the past. But the past was set in cement, impervious to guilt and regret and desperate wishes. There was nothing to do now but go on with the show. There were now two weeks left in The Count.

15

Marlon Grey stood across from Laura's door. His hand gripped the pistol under his coat. He was starting to feel dizzy; his legs were as weak as matchsticks. All of the acts had finished for the night, and Marlon knew from scouting out the club that Laura usually stayed late working. The moment had finally come. He could not turn back now. It was time to make things right.

Marlon had only casually followed The Count; it honestly did not matter to him who won and who lost. Then he saw the medical records revealing Laura's abortion. She did not even have the decency to leave town after her secret had been publicized; she just went on with her life as if she had done nothing more than have her gallbladder removed. The blind rage built within Marlon like an insidious tumor. Too many women had gotten away with it; he could not let this one simply walk away and go on with her life.

Laura finally emerged from her office; she adjusted her purse strap on her shoulder and looked up. She froze like an ice statue when she saw Marlon.

"Who are y—"

"Never mind who I am. It doesn't matter to you," Marlon responded, drawing his gun from his waistband.

Laura startled, her eyes engorged with fear and panic.

"Scared are you, Laura? Imagine how that innocent little baby felt as it was being ripped to pieces."

Laura caught her breath. "Are you talking about—"

Marlon peered at her. "Don't, Laura—just don't. You know what I'm talking about. And you know why I'm here," he said flatly.

Laura gaped at Marlon. Seconds passed in a vacuum devoid of sense or logic.

"You sluts aren't bleeding to death on kitchen tables anymore, so it is up to the honorable among us to make things right."

"Please don't do this," Laura implored in a desperate whisper.

"*You* didn't think twice about taking a life, did you, Laura?"

Laura looked him squarely in the eyes. "Yes, keep talking about honor, about valuing life, while you are pointing a gun at me."

"Shut up, *shut up!*" Marlon commanded, his bottom lip trembling with fear and anger.

"Go on, do your honorable duty, then go home and tuck your children into bed. Just make sure to wash the blood off your hands first."

"And what about you, Laura? Are *your* hands clean?"

Laura momentarily cast her eyes down but forced herself to meet Marlon's eyes again. Her gaze softened slightly. "I don't know. Maybe they aren't. Maybe I deserve to be punished." She paused and resumed her intrepid glare. "But not like this—not by you."

"Oh, God, right? I can't wait for Him. I—" Marlon stopped abruptly and darted his eyes to a shadowy figure slowly materializing from the hallway leading to the kitchen.

It was Emmon. Laura looked at him. She had not seen him up close in weeks. His face was drawn. Tiny red vessels ringed his eyes. His shoulders slumped.

"Leave her alone. You want your pound of flesh, take it from me," Emmon implored in a hoarse, strained voice.

Marlon furrowed his eyebrows. "Why? You haven't done anything."

"I've done plenty."

Marlon gulped hard. "Just stay right there, Mims," he ordered, his voice quavering more with each syllable.

Emmon inched closer. "Take me. Get out of here, Laura."

Laura stood in stunned silence. Marlon's finger froze on the trigger.

"Come on, hero. Take me."

"I'm warning you, Mims—*don't come any closer.*"

Emmon surged. Marlon, in blind survival mode, pulled the trigger.

Marlon gazed at Emmon lying on the floor, blood cascading from his heart like a scarlet waterfall. This is what it was to murder another human being, to take a life. So much mess for simply pulling a trigger, so much different than how it looked in the movies. Being a martyr was not as glamorous as it was cracked up to be. Marlon's legs suddenly sprouted a mind of their own; he wheeled around and bolted out the side door next to Laura's office.

Laura kneeled down next to Emmon. She put her hand over his heart and pressed hard, blood seeping through her fingers.

"Laura."

Laura looked up at Emmon.

"Dickens told me he was going to tell people about the abortion unless I dropped out of the contest, but I didn't. I just couldn't."

Laura stared at Emmon, the cold realization slowly descending upon her.

"I thought I was being strong."

Laura looked down at the cold, hard floor.

"I'm sorry, Laura. I couldn't walk away—I just couldn't lose," Emmon murmured as tears pooled in his eyes.

"I think this definitely disqualifies you," Laura whispered with a watery laugh.

Emmon managed a weak smile. "At least I can die a man." He looked squarely at Laura. "I love you, Laura. But I know now that wasn't enough."

A tear trickled down Laura's flushed face. She looked up and squeezed Emmon's hand. "I—"

"I knew I would end up losing to Bill," Emmon tittered, his eyelids drooping heavily.

Laura's tender smile disappeared; she stared blankly at Emmon. His final words on this earth were about losing. Laura watched as Emmon took his last breath, went to her office to call the police, and then sat with Emmon until they arrived. She told the officers what had happened and then walked outside through the front door.

Word had quickly spread around town. Laura saw Mack McGraw and Freddy Flagstaff standing just outside the yellow tape cordoning off the club, looking dazed and confused. What do you say to people who have lost their hero, a man who had breathed hope into their deflated lives? Laura was out of words by this point. She saw Russ leaning against the front wall of the club to her right. She walked over to him.

"I'm sorry, Russ; I should've called you right away. I wasn't thinking straight."

Russ shrugged his right shoulder. "Kind of glad you didn't; I hate blood."

Laura scoffed. "Except when it gets publicity for the club."

Russ furrowed his eyebrows but remained silent.

"Do they know who the guy is?" Laura queried, slightly deflated over her failed attempt to bait her boss.

"One of the cops said he turned himself in a little while ago. Said he looked at his kids' pictures on the mantel when he raced through the front door, felt sick to his stomach. His wife came to the police station with him. His name is Marlon Grey. I guess he's a member of some pro-life organization." Russ paused as he watched two young attendants in crisp white slacks load Emmon's body into the coroner's van. "Some pro-lifer," he muttered.

"No life is defined by just one act," Laura murmured as she looked down at the ground.

Russ stared thoughtfully at the bag containing Emmon's body. "Maybe we should put his head on a stake and plant it in the middle of the stage."

"I don't think so. This is already way too real for these people."

"I don't think there is anything worse than the death of a hero," Russ murmured as he gazed at Freddy Flagstaff and Mack McGraw.

Laura looked up at Russ, a reproachful glare marring her beautiful face. "Emmon was never a hero to you. He was your pawn—they all were."

Russ looked at Laura and smiled ruefully. "You still don't get it, do you Laura? All I did was start a competition. After that it was all up to the people. This town tore itself apart."

Laura stared at Russ for a moment and then looked down. "Maybe so." She lifted her head up again, her eyes red and misty. "But I didn't think it would end like this."

"End? My dear, it is only just beginning for Emmon. Nothing

makes for immortal fame like dying young and tragically."

Laura smiled slightly then turned around and walked back to her office.

Randy Yellowmander directed his photographer to get a good shot of Emmon's body bag before the attendants slammed the van doors shut. He had wanted a picture of Emmon's bloody body, but the police would not let him past the sacred yellow tape sealing off the crime scene. He decided a picture of the town's fallen hero in a plain black body bag would satisfy people's morbid appetites almost as well. Readership would definitely be up the next few weeks, and most definitely during Marlon Grey's trial. If Randy was not going to be able to ride Emmon's back to New York City, he could at least leech off his blood for a while.

With still no confession and no evidence, the burglary at Laura Hemmings's apartment remains unsolved.

The Count continued until the end of June, just as planned. Bill Dickens was officially declared the winner at the beginning of July. Emmon's fans chafed at Bill's victory but found some consolation in the fact that Emmon had died a hero, even if he was protecting a woman many people in town still despised.

Everyone had won. No one had won.
And The Count started again in July.
And Jada McKinna is still missing.

ACKNOWLEDGMENTS

I am immensely grateful to my family and friends for their constant and unwavering support during good times and bad; without you all, this book would not have been possible. Thank you, Mom, Dad, Bill Cute, Bridgette Harper, Kelly Chartier and Brett Parmenter; I am forever in your debt.

I would also specifically like to thank Bill Cute—still the best teacher ever—for reading and providing invaluable feedback on early drafts of my manuscript.

And thank you to the wonderful support team at BookBaby for helping to make this book a reality.